DEATH IN THE COVERTS

For hundreds of years, the Decker family has lived at Hurstley Place in Kent. In today's hard times, they are still a great family, although nowadays the pheasant shoot is financed and enjoyed by the members of a syndicate.

A pheasant drive at Hurstley Place ends in the discovery that a member of the syndicate has been shot dead—but this is only the first of three tragedies...

DEATH IN THE COVERTS

DEATH IN THE COVERTS

by
Roderic Jeffries

Dales Large Print Books
Long Preston, North Yorkshire,
England.

British Library Cataloguing in Publication Data.

Jeffries, Roderic
    Death in the coverts.

A catalogue record for this book is
available from the British Library

ISBN 1-85389-455-9 pbk

First published in Great Britain by W. Collins Ltd., 1966

Copyright © 1966 by Roderic Jeffries

Published in Large Print 1994 by arrangement with the copyright holder.

All rights reserved. No part of this publication may be reproduced, stored in a retrieval system, or transmitted in any form or by any means, electronic, mechanical, photocopying, recording or otherwise, without the prior permission of the Copyright owner.

Dales Large Print is an imprint of
Library Magna Books Ltd.
Printed and bound in Great Britain by
T.J. Press (Padstow) Ltd., Cornwall, PL28 8RW.

CHAPTER 1

Three cars arrived together as if in convoy. They turned off the road, came down the drive through the park and across the cattle-grid into the garden and halted half-way round the circular turning drive in front of the main entrance of Hurstley Place. Between the three of them, a Buick Riviera, a Ford Thunderbird, and a Dodge shooting-brake, they stretched a quarter of the way around the circular turning drive. The drivers climbed out and studied each other's shooting-suits, stockings, and boots.

' 'Morning, Joe,' said Rafferty. ' 'Morning, Phil.'

' 'Morning, Bill,' replied Abbotts. 'Good day for the birds, eh?'

They looked up at the sky which was temporarily almost free of clouds. There was a strong wind and as they watched a pigeon flew over them downwind. It flashed across the lawn and out of sight over the roof of the wing of the house.

'They'll be fast and furious today and no mistake,' said Abbotts. He laughed, a booming sound that suggested pints of beer. 'We'll be dead lucky if we hit anything.'

'And the birds will be unluckily dead?' said Wade.

Abbotts looked quickly at Wade to make out if this was meant to be funny.

'They'll hit 'em,' said Rafferty. He jerked his head in the direction of the house, behind him. 'This is just the kind of day they want because it lets 'em show us what brilliant shots they are.'

'I'll tell you one thing, I wouldn't say no to being half as good as either of 'em.' Abbotts put his hands in his pockets and jingled some coins.

'You can't help being good if you've shot all your life.'

'I don't know I agree,' said Wade.

Rafferty looked at the small, precise, thin-lipped man. 'You make a habit of not agreeing,' he retorted aggressively. 'You'll find that sometimes it doesn't bloody well matter whether you do or don't agree.'

'And no doubt you'll discover that sometimes people count their chickens before they've even collected the eggs.'

Abbotts tried, in his usual blundering style, to damp down the expressed dislike of the two men for each other. 'I reckon any man can reach a certain skill in shooting and then if he's not a born shot he won't get no further, no matter whether he practises every day for a year.'

'Are you speaking from the standpoint of an expert?' asked Wade, with heavy sarcasm.

'He didn't shoot so bad last time,' snapped Rafferty.

Wade smiled disdainfully. 'By what standards? Yours or the Deckers'?'

A Chevrolet Impala came round the circular lawn and parked behind the Dodge. Cranleigh climbed out. 'A good morning to one and all,' he said. He was a tall, thin man who dressed exactly as fashion dictated. He was often known as The Tailor's Dummy. 'How's the missus, Bill?'

'She's all right,' muttered Rafferty.

'How very thoughtful of you to ask,' said Wade. His cold, blue eyes looked from Cranleigh to Rafferty. 'Our Charlie's a very thoughtful sort, isn't he?'

'What's it matter to you what he is?'

'Asking after your wife shows a nice

spirit. When your wife's so lovely a lady as Daphne it's gentlemanly to ask after her health to show how concerned one is with it.'

Abbotts sniggered and brushed his bushy moustache with his right forefinger. Cranleigh had a way with women and it was said that his way had extended as far as Daphne Rafferty. Abbotts didn't really believe the story because Rafferty was a man who protected his possessions with every ounce of his cunning, but it was an amusing thought. It could mean that Rafferty wasn't always successful.

Cranleigh tried to look both flattered and indignant at the suggestion. He took a handkerchief from his pocket and carefully wiped his lips.

'Here, how about some booze to warm us up?' asked Abbotts, breaking the silence. 'There's whisky, rum, or brandy to gladden the cockles of your hearts and make your barrels straight.' He walked back to the Ford Thunderbird, opened the boot, and brought out a large pigskin case. Inside the case there were three silver flasks and half a dozen silver tumblers. 'Come on, you lucky lads, it's on the house. If you're T.T you can add some water.'

Cranleigh came across. 'I'll take a brandy, Joe, neat. It's not all that warm standing around, even with my waistcoat on.'

Abbotts had already noticed the waistcoat, but had deliberately not remarked on it. It was brightly coloured and did not seem to complement the suit, but if Cranleigh wore the combination it would only be because he had discovered it was 'right' to wear it. Abbotts decided to have a word with his London tailor on the subject.

Rafferty and Wade joined them at the car and each man chose brandy. Abbotts raised his silver tumbler. 'Here's cheers, dears. I reckon you'll find it's not a bad *vino*. I told my wine merchant I wanted nothing but the best.'

'A man of taste,' said Wade.

Abbotts shrugged his shoulders. Wade never missed the chance to make some dirty, snide remark. Anyway, he was hardly in any position to talk since the last trump would sound before he ever offered even cooking brandy. It hurt Wade to spend as much as a halfpenny.

A Morris 1000 Traveller came round the drive and parked behind the Chevrolet. In comparison with the other four cars it looked almost like a toy. A heavily-built, but not fat, man stepped out. He was dressed in a shooting-suit that had seen a great deal of wear and both elbows of the coat were leather patched. ' 'Morning, everyone,' he called out. 'Good day for the high birds.' He turned and climbed the three stone steps up to the porch, built with four pillars in the traditional English Renaissance style.

The four men by the car watched the newcomer open the front door and go into the house.

'They've not once asked us inside,' said Cranleigh, rather plaintively.

'You're not saying you really expect an invitation?' queried Wade.

'Well, it's our money that runs the shoot.'

'You'd have to be stupid to think that's a good reason to get you inside.'

Rafferty spoke belligerently. 'Well, isn't it?'

'If you don't understand, no explanation of mine'll help.'

'Are you setting yourself up as an authority?'

'I possess my native wits.'

'So does everyone else.'

'Then everyone else will know why they're never going to be invited inside.'

'Just have a think on this one, Mr Bloody Expert. It won't be long before I'm in there.'

'You flatter to deceive yourself.'

'I'm telling you, me and the missus are going to be invited.'

'Why get so het-up about the ridiculously impossible?'

'Impossible nothing. If you're so certain, have a bet on it.'

'I'm far too honest to bet on certainties.'

'More likely scared of losing.'

Rafferty and Wade stared at each other with a hatred neither man made any effort to hide.

Cranleigh spoke again, more plaintively than before. 'It's not as though we don't know how to behave.'

Wade chuckled.

Inside the house the newcomer, Henry Decker, crossed the hall to the left and went into the gun-room. His cousin, Julian Decker, was cleaning out any traces of oil from the barrels of two guns. ' 'Morning, Julian. It's just about perfect conditions, isn't it?'

'Hallo, Henry. I had a word with Adams

earlier on and he promised the birds would come over King's Beat like bullets.'

'Has he managed to hold the birds this season? With all the fine weather in September and October, most estates have lost a hell of a lot from straying.'

'He's done damned well, but you wouldn't think so to listen to him. Still, he's a lot around and knows it because he's gone as far as to suggest a bag of three hundred today.'

'Has he, by God! I'm going to need all the cartridges I've brought along.'

'There'll be plenty in reserve. The four Mustavabeers always bring enough for the whole season.' Julian smiled. 'Maybe they've got shares in the cartridge manufacturers.' He was a tall man and lean, with the hard leanness of someone who carried out a considerable amount of manual exercise. His face was the typical long narrow Decker face. 'Are all four of them here yet?'

'They're outside, swigging liquor. Damned if I couldn't have done with something strong, but never an offer from them. I must say that instead of parking my battered car behind their posh ones I thought I ought to go round to the tradesmen's entrance.'

The door opened and a man in a wheelchair came into the gun-room.

' 'Morning, Fawcett,' said Henry Decker. 'How's life?'

'Not so bad, Henry, all things considered. At least I can still shoot.' Fawcett, the elder son, had been physically normal until he was five years old and then he had contracted Mail's Disease, a progressive atrophying of muscles in the back and thighs. By seven he was permanently confined to a wheel-chair and the doctors said he could not live to be twenty. When he was twenty, the doctors said there was no hope of his living to be twenty-five. When he was thirty, the doctors finally admitted that they could offer no prognosis.

Julian lifted up the gun, broken, so that he could look down the barrels. 'Not a speck of oil left. It's all ready for you, Fawcett.' He went round the table and handed the gun to his brother.

Fawcett closed the gun and then raised it to his shoulder several times, taking the far light as his point of aim. He had very broad shoulders and large hands, as if to compensate for the pitiful weakness of the lower half of his body. 'How many cartridges are we going to need, Julian?'

'I'll shove a hundred in the bag for you. You won't need more than that for the first three beats unless Adams has been lying more than usual about the number of birds.'

'Adams is a first-class keeper with the sense to realise that the boss always expects more than he's told to.' Fawcett slid his gun into the leather case strapped to the side of the wheel-chair. 'We'd better be moving. You know what a martinet Adams is for starting on time.' He led the way out of the room, manoeuvring the chair with skilful ease. Henry Decker followed and Julian brought up the rear, two empty cartridge bags over his left shoulder, a case of 400 cartridges under his arm, his gun, broken, over the crook of his other arm, and a cartridge belt round his waist.

Two women entered the hall. Lydia Decker, the mother of Fawcett and Julian, was a woman of sixty-five. With her was Barbara Harmsworth, Julian's fiancée, dressed in sweater and slacks.

'Good morning, Henry,' said Lydia. 'It's so nice to see you as I wasn't expecting to. It was only at breakfast this morning that

I asked Julian how you were.'

Fawcett spoke impatiently. 'We told you half a dozen times that Henry was coming out today.'

'Did you, dear? Never mind, it's very nice to see him. Henry, you've put on weight and need to take more exercise. During most of my marriage, we went riding every day for at least half an hour before breakfast and I'm sure that's why neither of us ever put on fat. I was reading in a magazine only yesterday...'

'You'll have to tell him some other time, Mother,' interrupted Julian. 'We're due to get moving. I promised Adams we'd be at the duck-stand by a quarter to ten at the very latest.'

'Are you staying to supper, Henry?' she asked.

'Thanks very much, but I must get home. Clara isn't too well just at the moment.'

'She must stop fussing about her health, Henry. Almost all illness comes from fussing. Bring her to dinner and I'll ask the Bellfonts and...'

'Some other time, Mother,' said Julian and led the way out of the house.

Barbara smiled at Lydia. 'You'll never

get any sense out of them if they think they're holding up Adams. Are you coming out today?'

'I don't think I will. With everyone out of the way, I'll have a chance to get on with some work.'

Barbara was about to suggest she should forget all the work for once, but stopped herself. If Lydia Decker slaved in the house it was because she wanted to. True to the Decker traditions, the house had become a monument for her, perhaps even an idol that needed constant idolising. Hurstley Place *was* the Deckers: it was difficult, even impossible, to imagine one without the other.

Barbara put on thornproof coat and leggings and went round to the kennels to collect Toby, her G.S.P dog which she used for picking-up.

★ ★ ★ ★

Adams, head keeper, shouted at the line of beaters to halt and cursed them for a shower of ignorant pikies. 'Keep in a straight line and keep them sticks tapping or the birds'll go back.'

'There ain't no birds to go anywhere,'

said the beater next to Adams. 'They've all been poached.'

Adams cursed the beater. On shooting days, he worried himself almost into his grave. The old hands knew this and took great delight in adding to his worries. He cursed again. It was all right for them to laugh and not worry if only a handful of birds went over the guns, but the entire responsibility for the success of the shoot was his. 'Get moving,' he shouted. 'And keep them sticks tapping.'

The line of thirty-five beaters moved forward. Adams called his Labrador back as it tried to work too far forward. He slashed a patch of brambles with his stick and a hen pheasant erupted out of them, struck the branches of a tree with beating wings, cleared the trees and then swung left. Adams violently waved his hands to try to turn the bird back, but without any success. He swore. If all the birds turned too soon with the wind, none would cross the guns. Yet this should be the best beat of the day.

One of the grammar school boys went forward, out of line, to chase a squirrel which had scurried along the ground and into a rabbit hole. Adams roughly ordered him back into the line. It wasn't like the old days, he angrily told himself as he slowly moved forward in a zig-zag, beating the undergrowth and tapping the trees. In the old days, men were only too glad to be beaters and they worked at the job, without talking or smoking, or jeering at the head keeper: nowadays, twenty-five shillings and a pint of beer weren't enough to bring in the men and numbers had to be made up from schoolkids who didn't, or wouldn't, understand and learn the skills of beating. Put a boy out as a stop and in five minutes he became so bored that he moved on and all the birds escaped.

There was a flurry of gunfire which quickly died away. Adams looked as far along the line of beaters as he could see. What had caused that flush of birds? Was Jim, the under-keeper, doing his job at the other end of the line? Jim was always looking for an excuse to down-tools and have a smoke, saying these were the days of less work for more cash and what the hell was the use of killing oneself for the wealthy bastards who went shooting. It wasn't any good being a keeper if one thought like that. Keepers worked all day and all night, if necessary, because that was the only way of doing a good job.

Adams ploughed through a thick patch of brambles which scraped along his thorn-proof leggings and caught at the feet of his boots. A melanistic cock pheasant, with a glorious green sheen, ran out of the far side of the brambles and away towards the rhododendrons, which was in the right direction. The Labrador looked eagerly at the running bird, but did not chase.

The beaters reached the rhododendron bushes. Soon, the main flushes of birds would begin as the vanguard came up against the flushing fence: soon, Adams would be able to judge from the intensity of gunfire how many birds were going over the guns. There should be a good showing, but at the back of every honest keeper's mind was always the fear that the night before a shoot the commercial poachers had been into the coverts or that a plague of foxes had suddenly materialised.

He pushed his way between two rhododendron bushes. Ahead of him were several pheasants, undecided what to do. He tapped one of the bushes and they ran ahead. His Labrador put up a rabbit, but again did not chase.

The gunfire started, but his trained ears

immediately picked out the fact that only the guns on the left were firing. He looked up at the sky to confirm what he already knew; the high wind was coming from the west and would be taking the birds with it. Numbers 4, 5, 6 and 7 guns would be getting almost all the shooting. Mr Julian had been number 5 at the last beat so he would be number 7 at this one. That was good. He'd bring the birds down. Mr Julian wasn't the best shot in the country, but he was very, very useful. He could really take the high, curling birds. Today, he'd get all the high, curling birds he could want.

There was a flush of birds from just ahead and Adams called the line to hold. The beaters came to a stop, tapping their sticks as they waited for the flush to finish. A woodcock side-slid between the trees, like some restless phantom. Some of the boys shouted, ' 'Cock, 'Cock right.' Their excited shouts caused a second and premature flush of pheasants. Adams swore. Was nothing going to go right?

After a while, he called the beaters forward and as they cleared the rhododendron bushes and started to beat the ash trees, Adams was able to check that the line was reasonably straight. There was another flush of birds, and another. The line of beaters held each time. The birds were rising to tree level and then swerving and curling left at ever increasing speed, wings frantically beating until the birds had gained enough height to plane. From the ash trees, Adams could see the birds as they crossed the guns, who were invisible to him. Number 7 was really pulling them out of the sky. It was beautiful shooting and Adams decided, in a burst of generosity, that Mr Julian was still improving. Number 6 didn't seem to be doing anything. The birds were crossing where number 6 should be and weren't even being shot at. That was odd. Mr Julian usually made certain even the stupidest gun knew enough to stay at his stick. Number 5 was making a lot of noise and achieving nothing, the birds going over him quite unscathed. That meant number 5 was one of the four Mustavabeers. In the old days, men like them would never have been seen on a proper shoot. Each of them tipped him £30 at the end of the season, but that didn't mean they'd bought either his liking or his respect.

As the flush was over, he called the

beaters on again. Only two paces farther on, another flush began and this became a major one with more and more birds rising. The press of birds was so great that now some of them were going off to the right, but even so the wind was bringing them down and away from numbers 1 and 2. He watched the main stream of birds swerve out to the left and for a few seconds he allowed himself the pleasure of a certain amount of self-satisfaction. This was the best lot of birds he could ever remember at this beat and they were flying as well as they had ever done.

When only one or two birds were rising, Adams called the line on and they continued through to the flushing fence. There was one last heavy flush, of brief duration, and then the beat was over.

He stepped over the wire-netting flushing-fence and raised the lower half so that the birds could walk underneath. He shouted at the beaters to raise the fence right along its length and made his way between the very old pollard ash and willow trees which, he'd been told, were of great historical value. The undergrowth of dead bracken and trailing brambles was very heavy. A hen pheasant rose up at his feet and, flying very low, crossed to the Larch Plantation. The Labrador watched it until it was out of sight. Even now, after all his years keepering, it still amazed him how pheasants would 'freeze' next-door to the guns and only move if directly disturbed. Could they possibly realise that their point of greatest safety was next to their point of greatest danger?

He reached number 7 stand, marked by a stick with a Gilbertson and Page numbered plastic tag and by over sixty empty cartridge cases. Adams was glad that Mr Julian had had the best shooting, not just because he was the best shot but because it was only fitting that it should fall to a Decker.

Julian came round a pollard willow whose trunk was so ancient and gnarled that it was easy to believe it might have supplied some of the bows used at Agincourt. He held a brace of birds in each hand. 'You excelled yourself, Adams. I'll never have a better stand than that one.'

'I thought it might be useful, Mr Julian.'

'The place was alive with birds and did you see how they flew? Like beserk mosquitoes. I've thirty-four down and every one worth two anywhere else. If you see Miss Harmsworth and I don't, ask her to come up here with her dog, will you?'

'Yes, sir. I didn't hear much from number six, yet the birds was seeming to be going over him.'

'He must have had as many as I did. Number six? That must have been Mr Rafferty. Maybe his gun jammed, or something.'

'Or maybe the birds were just too difficult for him,' muttered Adams, with the freedom of speech of someone who had worked for the same family for over thirty years.

He pushed his way through the brambles and bracken towards number 6 stand. The Labrador found a dead cock pheasant and brought it to him. He hurriedly bent down and took it. His dog was first-class in the line, but was not the softest mouthed retriever in the world. He called out to Mr Julian that he had picked that bird. One pace farther on was a small cloud of feathers but no dead bird, which meant a runner. Miss Harmsworth's dog would find that. He had no time for new-fangled dogs, and German ones at that, but even he had to admit that her German Shorthaired

Pointer was a good picker-up.

He went round another gnarled and twisted willow tree, split by lightning years ago but still alive, and came in sight of number 6 stand. It was immediately apparent why Rafferty had not been shooting. He lay on the ground, half doubled-up, with a very messy wound in his head.

CHAPTER 2

Julian drove the Land-Rover along the ride until he braked to a halt by the Hengist Oak. 'It's just across there,' he said, pointing to the right of a pollard willow.

Doctor Gooden climbed out of the Land-Rover. 'Is this chap Rafferty any connection with the man in Avonley who's built up a chain of electrical stores all over the place?'

'The same.'

'Reputation says he's not one of the world's most charming men?'

'It's no secret that I'd rather not have

him, or his friends, in the shoot.' Julian took a cigarette case from his pocket and offered it. The doctor shook his head. 'You know how things are these days, though. The shoot costs something over two and a half thousand a year to run and the money has to come from somewhere.'

The doctor made no comment. He was old enough to have seen almost from the beginning the social revolution which had resulted, amongst other things, in men like Rafferty being able to buy guns in shoots which before had been privately and exclusively run. The doctor did not think the change was at all a bad thing: he had also seen the poverty in the towns and, to a lesser extent, in the countryside and he hoped never again to witness such an evil. But he had an instinctive respect—in no way subservient—for families such as the Deckers, who had lived on the same land for hundreds of years and he could understand how reluctant Julian was to have to deal with men like Rafferty. 'Where is he?'

'Straight through. Look out for the brambles, though. Some of them would tear holes in a suit of armour.'

Julian led the way through the undergrowth to the stand where Rafferty's body lay. The doctor looked at the body for a while and then knelt down by it. 'There's obviously nothing I can do here. What the hell d'you think happened?'

'He must have stumbled over something. It never filtered through to him that a gun was any more lethal than a walking stick. When he first came here I tried to be tactful about the way he waved it around, but tact wasn't any use and I had to get rude. Before Fawcett and I were ever allowed to fire a gun we had to carry an empty one around for six months to teach us to respect it.'

'How is your brother?' asked the doctor, as he stood up.

'I think the pain's been worse, but you know what he is. It only annoys him if you start trying to help.'

'Was he out shooting today?'

'He wouldn't miss a day for anything. He says he'll have to be screwed down in his coffin before he quits.'

'He's got guts.' From Doctor Gooden, that was a very great compliment. He stared at the body. 'I take it you've been in touch with the police?'

'I've reported it and told them you were coming along.' Julian flicked the ash from his cigarette. 'Did he die instantly?'

'As instantly as anyone dies, which is an imponderable. The shot must have messed up a fair proportion of his brains. What kind of family is there?'

'He's married, but I've never heard of any children.'

They returned to the Land-Rover. Julian backed up the ride to the cross-ride and then turned into the cross-ride which led to the field.

When they reached Hurstley Place, the doctor left the Land-Rover and went over to his car after saying good-bye. He drove round the circular raised lawn and across the cattle-grid. As the grid rattled to the passage of the tyres he tried to imagine how Rafferty had been holding the gun to have shot himself. He concluded that Rafferty had been extraordinarily careless; quite extraordinarily careless.

Back at the house, Julian crossed the hall to the small hall-like passage beyond off which led the two withdrawing-rooms and the dining-room. He went into the red withdrawing-room, large enough to house a full size billiards-table in one corner.

On the walls hung most of the family portraits, none by famous artists but all by artists of reasonable merit: even the most cursory inspection of the paintings showed how the long narrow face had been with the Deckers from the time of Charles the Second.

Barbara, a glass of sherry in one hand, stood to the left of the fireplace and Fawcett sat in his wheel-chair to the right of it. In the fireplace, ten feet wide with an elaborately carved stone mantelpiece, burned several thick logs. The heat from the fire was very soon lost in the large room. A visiting American had once said, in mid winter, that history was wonderful, but central heating was more wonderful.

'Has Gooden gone?' asked Fawcett.

'I suggested a drink, but he said he hadn't time,' answered Julian.

'Did he know what would happen now?' asked Barbara.

Julian crossed to the table in the corner on which were two decanters and several glasses. He poured himself out a sherry. 'The police will be along any minute: they'll handle everything.'

'It's...it's rather horrible.'

'On the contrary,' replied Fawcett, 'for

the first time it inclines me to believe in divine justice. For four years he's been waving his gun around and at last he's discovered why that's a bad habit.'

'But that doesn't stop this being horrible, Fawcett.'

'My dear Barbara, learn to rejoice at the joyful things in life.'

She looked quickly at Julian. She liked Fawcett, except when he was in a black mood such as he was in at the moment. Even then, she tried always to remember that any man who suffered as Fawcett did must have black moods. Nevertheless, her nature was such that she could not understand his viewing the death with anything but compassion.

Knowing how she felt, Fawcett perversely continued the conversation. 'He has paid up everything for the shoot, hasn't he, Julian?'

'Yes,' replied Julian.

'Then we now have his money, but not him. I couldn't have suggested a better arrangement if I'd tried.'

'Lay off it, Fawcett.'

'Lay off what?'

'Can't you see you're upsetting Barbara?'

Fawcett propelled his chair across to

the corner and helped himself to another drink. Sometimes, the injustices of life gripped him by the throat and threatened to choke him. Barbara was attractive and desirable and his mind could savour such facts even though his body could not respond to them. Julian would marry her, make love to her, and enjoy life while he, Fawcett, if he lived, would be tied to his wheel-chair: a hulk of flesh that was called a man, but which had few manly attributes. He drank the sherry as quickly as he could and poured himself a third one. Rafferty had been a crude, obnoxious pig of a man, but he had been a man. He had had a wife.

Julian watched the way in which his brother was drinking. Often, Fawcett reacted to a black mood by drinking heavily. From the way in which he had just looked at Barbara, Julian could guess she was the innocent cause of much of the present mood. He wondered how Fawcett would react to his and Barbara's marriage in four months' time.

'Give me a cigarette, Julian,' asked Barbara.

He offered her one and took one himself. 'How did Toby work?'

'Not too badly,' she answered dully.

'Old Bowker said he had a very good runner at the first beat?'

'It was quite a good one.'

He moved to her side and took hold of her free hand. 'Cheer up, darling.'

She managed to smile very briefly. 'I'm sorry to be like some prophet of doom, but it's horrible knowing I'd spoken to him only a short time before. He wasn't a very nice man, but I had a few words with him and then...' She gripped his fingers.

'Aren't we told that in the midst of life we are in death?' demanded Fawcett.

Julian was about to reply angrily, but he checked himself. 'Where's Mother?' he asked.

'In the kitchen, getting lunch. She said that you had to have a proper meal now that you weren't going to eat in the keeper's cottage,' said Barbara.

'She needn't have bothered. We've still got all the cold meat and sandwiches.'

'You must know your mother better than that, Julian. If her two beloved sons aren't tucking into an eight course meal whenever they're at home, she reckons they're well on the way to dying from starvation.'

'Then couldn't the Danellis have done it?'

'They had the day off as it's a shooting day...' She stopped. Abruptly, she had reminded herself of what had happened.

★ ★ ★ ★

The police car followed a Pledge's lorry down the A20 to the Henton cross-roads and then turned right on to the back road to the coast. Detective Inspector Doherty, driving, tried to clear the inside of the misted-up windscreen with the back of his hand, but succeeded only in making smears. 'There's a cloth in the cubbyhole in front of you, sir, if you wouldn't mind.'

The uniformed superintendent opened the glove locker and brought out a tattered yellow duster. He cleared the screen in front of himself and then carefully put the duster in the D.I's lap. 'It sounds nasty.'

'And messy.'

'That's not the way I meant it.'

Doherty knew very well how Superintendent Earnest meant it: to use a timeworn, but also time-honoured, pun, he meant it earnestly. He was a worrier which was why he had suffered from a duodenal ulcer before he became a station inspector and why he was clearly about to start another one. He was worried because they were about to meet the Deckers. The Deckers were County and therefore, even in this age of equality, only to be handled with kid gloves.

'Tread lightly, won't you,' said the superintendent mournfully.

'Like Agag?'

'What's that?'

'He walked around on egg-shells.'

'For God's sake, stop talking nonsense.'

'Yes, sir.'

The superintendent looked at a parked car as they passed it. 'Of course...' He stopped as he turned round to stare at the car again, resumed speaking when he turned back. 'If it's only an accident, there's not much to do.'

'No, there isn't.'

'Just a few statements and that sort of thing. This Rafferty who shot himself?'

'Yes, sir?'

'Is he the bloke who runs that chain of electrical goods shops and God knows what else?'

'I expect so. He'd have the kind of

money you need to go shooting.'

'But surely they wouldn't have someone like him to their place?'

'Why not? If he hasn't actually learned to write, he can always sign his cheque with a cross.'

'God, man, your sense of humour stinks more and more.'

As a detective inspector who was not going to gain promotion before he retired in two years' time, Doherty felt he could afford the kind of sense of humour that annoyed his superiors.

He braked the car as they reached another cross-roads and turned right.

'D'you get on to the police surgeon?' asked Earnest.

'Yes, sir.'

'And the photographer?'

'He'll be standing by if needed, sir.' And so will Uncle Tom Cobbleigh and all, thought Doherty.

They became silent. The car, it was Doherty's and run on a mileage allowance, squeaked every time the near-side springs rode up or down. 'Aren't we nearly there?' asked Doherty, as they passed through the village of Fordton, a small collection of houses, a pub, and a general store.

'Yes,' replied Earnest gloomily. 'It's along here on the right. Big pair of gates: you can't miss 'em.'

Doherty saw the wrought-iron gates and braked the car to a halt as he waited for an oncoming lorry to pass. He turned into the park.

At first they could see nothing but the flanking elm trees, then the drive bore round to the right and they came in sight of the house. Doherty's first reaction was one of amused incredulity that anyone should choose to live in such a pile of a mansion. It was big enough, and bleak enough, to house a regiment and the wing looked to his entirely uneducated eyes like some hastily tacked-on folly, with its arched and mullioned windows which had no counterpart in the main building.

He drove across the cattle-grid, half-way round the circular lawn, and parked in front of the massive porch. He noticed the superintendent run his finger round the inside of his collar, as if it had suddenly become too tight.

They left the car, climbed the three stone steps, and went between the two central columns of the porch to the heavy wooden door. Doherty banged the ponderous knocker on the iron stud. He stepped back a pace, looked up, and saw above the door a crest, carved in stone. If the Dohertys had a crest it would consist of two potatoes and a poteen still.

The door was opened by an elderly, plumpish woman, wearing an apron over a colourless, saggy sweater and a very old tweed skirt. She was holding a silver candlestick which she had clearly been cleaning.

'We're the police,' said Doherty. 'Would you tell Mr Decker we're here.'

'Of course. Do come in and mind that little step there, so many people trip over it. Just wait here a second and I'll find Julian. I expect he's in the green withdrawing-room which I think is a lovely room, but nothing will warm it up at this time of year.'

Doherty tried to frame an apology for having so very obviously mistaken her for a maid, but wisely realised it was hopeless. As Mrs Decker left them, he looked at Earnest and was not in the least surprised to see the expression of anguished horror on the superintendent's face: no doubt Earnest was preparing himself for the firing squad.

Doherty looked round the hall. It was a large, flag-stoned room with a vast fireplace in which was burning what looked to be the best part of a tree. The fire gave off no appreciable heat and the hall felt colder than outside. Along the walls were a number of weapons, ranging from halberds to flintlock pistols, and in each of the far corners was a complete set of armour, the hands of which rested on the hilts of broadswords. Above the weapons and hung round the walls were heraldic shields of designs that increased in complexity.

A man, wearing a shooting-suit in a light heather mixture, came into the hall. 'Good morning. I'm Julian Decker.'

'Detective Inspector Doherty, sir, and this is Superintendent Earnest.'

Earnest half bowed.

'Let's go into the study.'

'Right, sir, but can I just check on one thing? Is anyone with the body now to see nothing's disturbed?'

'I've told my head keeper to see nothing's touched, so you've no worries.' Julian led the way from the hall to the smaller hall beyond, at the end of which was a flight of stairs. The study was on the right.

After they had had a drink and Julian

had given them a résumé of the facts, they left the house. Julian drove the Land-Rover and the detectives followed in their car until they reached the field before King's Beat. Here, the detectives left the car and climbed into the Land-Rover in which they crossed the field to the woods.

They walked down the ride and between the pollard ashes and willows to number 6 stand. The body of Rafferty lay half doubled up, in what was nearly a foetal position. Adams waited at the edge of the small circular clearing of the stand.

Julian looked at his watch. 'You won't want me around, will you?'

'No, sir, thank you,' replied Doherty. 'But I would be grateful if someone could stay with us in case we want some help.'

Julian spoke to Adams. 'Have you eaten yet?'

'No, sir, but there's no rush. If you'd just tell Latham he can take over from me when he's fed.'

'I'll do that.' Julian spoke to Doherty. 'Let me know if I can help in any way.'

'Thank you very much, sir.'

Julian turned and left. Doherty watched

him until he was out of sight and thought how difficult, perhaps impossible, it would be to mistake Julian Decker's position in life—yet there did not seem to be any arrogance in the man. Doherty was amused by his own train of thought. What had he been expecting: the traditional village squire, claiming his *droit de seigneur?*

He stood close to a willow and studied the scene. Rafferty appeared strangely peaceful until one looked at his head and then there was a bloody mess. Just beyond the body, lying on its side with the butt towards the body and the muzzles pointing away from it, was a double-barrel shotgun. Two feet to the right was a leather cartridge bag on which were stamped, in large gold letters, the initials W.R.

Doherty stepped across to the body. He looked down. The side of Rafferty's head, above the ear, had been blown in and it seemed as if the path of the shot had been level. This, in conjunction with the way the gun was lying, suggested it had been an unusual accident.

Doherty turned and spoke to the keeper. 'Had he been shooting for long?'

Adams hawked and spat. 'Him? Never

touched a gun 'til he was too old to know what to do with it.'

There would have been no love lost between Rafferty and Adams, thought Doherty. There was no snob so great as the man who had worked for a large family for a number of years and it was pretty obvious that Adams had been with the Deckers for some time. 'Was he often careless about how he handled a gun?'

'I've seen the size of his shot more times'n I can remember.'

'What d'you mean?' asked the superintendent.

Adams spoke scornfully. 'I mean he'd wave them barrels around so as you'd find yourself lookin' down 'em.'

'Then you're not surprised he shot himself?' asked Doherty.

'I'm just astonished it took so bloody long.'

Doherty looked more closely at the gun. He knew enough about shotguns to be able to judge that this was probably a best-London gun, but he put the question to Adams to make certain.

'Aye,' replied Adams, 'it's a real good 'un. A thousand quid, but he's so poor a shot I can shoot better with a twisted

Belgian than he could with that.'

'How long's he had it?'

'Asked me before his first season here what gun he ought to use. I told him something cheap, so as not to waste good money. Nothing cheap for him, though. He makes out he's a first-class shot and goes up to London for the best and wasn't he downright upset when they told him it'd take more'n a year for delivery.'

'You wouldn't really expect this quality of gun to go off accidentally, would you?'

'Anything'll go off wrong if you treat it wrong. Quality don't count for much if you're stupid.'

Doherty showed an endless patience. 'It looks in good order?'

'Should be.'

'If it is, surely it wouldn't easily go off accidentally?'

'Depends whether he had the safety on, don't it?'

Doherty walked round the gun until he could clearly see the upper part of the butt. The safety catch was forward on the off position. Suppose Rafferty had released the safety catch and been about to shoot at a bird when he tripped over, could he have suffered the kind of wound he had? The experts would answer that one.

Doherty stepped away from the gun. Once it had been photographed—obviously he was going to have to call the photographer in—he would break it and see which barrel had been fired. After that, he'd send it to a firearms expert to discover whether the mechanism was in good order. Long ago, Doherty had learned that whenever there was even the slightest possibility of doubt, the matter was best treated in its gravest light. If this proved to be an accident, then all that would be wasted would be a few photographs and the time of a few men.

The superintendent took off his peaked hat and scratched the bald patch on the top of his head. 'How many people were out shooting?'

'Just the seven,' replied Adams.

'What about you keepers: don't you carry guns?'

'You don't know much about shooting, do you? Keepers carrying guns on one of the days?'

Doherty briefly smiled, thereby dispelling his naturally gloomy expression. It would be more accurate to say that the superintendent knew absolutely nothing about covert shooting. He spoke to Adams. 'Do all the guns stand in a line here?'

'The woods come down in a V, like, and numbers two to seven stand round the V.'

'Not number one?'

'He starts back up the ride, well above number seven, and comes down with the beaters. When he reaches number seven, he walks right round the ride to take up position at his stand at number one.'

Doherty turned round and stared at the undergrowth. 'You can't see any ride from here.'

'You won't see nothing, and that's fact. I keep on to Mr Julian to have some of the rubbish cleared to help the pick-up, but there's always more important things for the woodmen.'

'D'you know who number one gun was?'

Adams scratched the side of his face. 'Mr Wade,' he said finally.

'So he'd have started right back and then when he reached the ride we came down on he'd have gone along it and right round?'

'That's it.'

'Would there have been anyone on the other side of the ride?'

'The pickers-up.'

'The what?' asked the superintendent.

Adams shrugged his shoulders wearily, as if unable to understand such ignorance.

'People with dogs, sir,' explained Doherty, 'who pick up the birds which are shot and land well back from the guns.'

'What a bloody how-d'you-do just to get a few birds for the pot,' muttered the superintendent.

Adams hawked and spat with great deliberation.

'Well?' said the superintendent.

'We'll have to go ahead with everything, sir, just for the moment.'

The superintendent shoved his hands into the pockets of his uniform mackintosh. 'It could easily have been a complete accident.'

'Yes, sir. But as of now it might almost as easily have been something else.'

The superintendent shook his head. Doherty was uncertain whether that meant the other didn't agree or whether it was an expression of regret that he had to agree.

CHAPTER 3

Following a quick lunch, and Barbara's departure, Julian walked round the house to the southern face. Here was his favourite vantage point. The southern face of the house was William and Mary and as the wind was hardly visible the house was reduced to pleasing proportions. During his mother's life it was quite impossible to alter the house because to do so would be to hurt her very much, but after her death he would have the Victorian wing, with its now anachronistic ballroom, knocked down and, if he could afford it, the top floor of the house removed. Thirty-one bedrooms had been a workable proposition in the days of servants galore, but in the present day so great a number meant only woodworm, rot, falling plaster, and decay. His mother still regularly dusted the twenty bedrooms on the top floor and polished the brass handles of the doors, as if some day they might again be inhabited, but it was a hopeless gesture. Not that this hopeless gesture was in any way pathetic. Lydia Decker was too genuine to be pathetic. She might revere the past and Hurstley Place beyond anything else, but underneath her apparent detachment from the world she seemed surprised to find herself in was a sharp mind and a natural ability to differentiate in a second a man from a rotter. That was why she had disliked Rafferty so much. Her dislike had grown when he had gushingly presented her with the most expensive transistor wireless on the market—he casually mentioned it was the most expensive—as a 'small token of my humble esteem and gratitude.' Rafferty always believed she disliked him because she was an insufferable snob: nothing would ever have persuaded him that she just plain disliked him. Rafferty had been a rotter, all right, but for a long time they hadn't realised just how much of a one: not, that was, until he started to blackmail them.

Julian leaned against the weathered bricks. He looked across the twenty-yard wide terrace at the stone balustrade and noticed one of the stone vases in front of the balustrade needed repairing. Then he looked beyond, at the park. A large flock of Romney Marsh sheep were grazing the ley that had been planted the previous autumn. Until his father had died, the park had never been cultivated and had always contained a large herd of fallow deer. One of the traditions of Hurstley Place had been the herd of deer, said to have been started back in 1473 when the family had lived in a castle a mile from the present house. His father had always said that if ever the deer went the Deckers would go, but after his father's death tradition had had to give way to practical farming. The park was almost two hundred and fifty acres, of which one hundred and fifty could be farmed. At a time when any and every family estate was threatened with extinction from one cause or another, every acre of land properly farmed was an insurance.

He jerked himself away from the wall, crossed to the balustrade, turned, and looked back at the house. From here, it appeared so much more friendly than from anywhere else: it became an overgrown home and not a mansion. It was frightening to think that if Rafferty had lived they might have lost it.

It was difficult to say exactly what

Rafferty's motives had been for his blackmail. It wasn't simply money, because Rafferty had been rich—not that any man said no to more than he had. But, again, it hadn't simply been a childish attempt to force his acceptance into a society he professed to despise, yet secretly longed to enter: though God knows why. Perhaps his motives had been a confused mixture of envy, hatred, greed, and the desire to prove he was really the better man.

Lydia Decker walked round the east corner of the house. She was wearing an old and patched coat over the apron she had put on as soon as lunch was finished. When she wasn't polishing, she was cleaning: when she wasn't cleaning, she was washing-down. Her sons had long since ceased to try to dissuade her from working so hard as they realised that this was all she wanted to do. She was rendering homage to Hurstley Place, built in 1692, alterations in 1735, additions in 1873, situated on land enfeoffed to the Lanchvilles in 1083 which had descended to the Deckers in 1254, confiscated from the Deckers in 1651 by the sobersides of The Commonwealth, restored to the Deckers in 1662 after merry Charles had been on the throne for a couple of years and had met Sarah Decker, whose portrait in the red withdrawing-room showed how attractive she had been.

'Aren't you cold, Julian?' asked Lydia, as she came to a halt. 'The wind's becoming very sharp. I told Barbara she should wear a thicker coat. These days, women go around in underwear that is worse than useless and it's no wonder they're always catching colds. They should wear woollen underwear...'

'Mother, can you imagine Barbara in long woollen combs?'

'She's used to that place of hers Julian, with central heating making it like a hot-house and when she comes to live here she'll just have to wear something warmer.'

'Then she probably will, but not long woollens.'

'I've been wondering whether to have just a little central heating put in The Red House. What do you think?'

'It's a good idea.' He wondered whether she would live for long once he was married and she had moved to the dower house? Most of her purpose for living would have gone. Yet when he and Barbara had tentatively, and very reluctantly, suggested she should continue to live at Hurstley, in a self-contained flat, she had refused.

She turned up the collar of her coat. 'Are you sure you're warm enough, dressed as you are?'

'Quite sure, thanks.'

'What are the police doing?'

'I left them in the woods and haven't seen anyone since.'

'Fawcett is in one of his moods, now.'

'Yes, I know.'

'The poor boy suffers so much. Julian, do you think it'll all come out about your father?'

'I don't see why it should.'

'But if they start finding out things...'

'Don't worry so, Mother.'

'I can't help worrying. I dreamt last night that the house had to be sold.'

'Rafferty was alive last night so your dream can hardly be relevant.'

'It was a premonition. I've told you time and time again that my Irish blood allows me premonitions. After all, my grandmother was granted a vision.'

'Your last premonition was the winner of the Derby. You backed it and lost all your five shillings.'

'Did I? Are you sure that was a premonition and not a tip?'

'Quite sure. You tried to persuade me to put a pound on it because it couldn't possibly lose as your premonitions were always true.'

'You could be right. You're usually so very practical.'

'Somebody around here has to be.' He tucked his arm round hers. 'Let's go inside. I'd better try and cope with the latest batch of agricultural returns.'

'I just cannot understand what they do with all the forms. Look at the number you have to fill in and send off and when you think of all the other farms in the country there must be...'

He ceased to listen. Her dream of losing Hurstley was one that she had quite often and it must express some of her deep-rooted fears: but this time it might truly be called a premonition. Everything depended on whether the police closely investigated Rafferty's past life and on how much evidence Rafferty had left lying around.

★ ★ ★ ★

Detective Inspector Doherty brought his Hillman, squeaking mournfully, to a halt before the front door of Rafferty's house. He climbed out. The wind flicked the ends of his hair where it was kept long to try to conceal the growing baldness. Mrs Rafferty was probably somewhere about the house, watching the television maybe. Everything in her world was fine. She lived in an expensive house, her husband was wealthy, life was easy. Now, she was going to be brought face to face with a gloomy D.I who would tell her, as gently as possible, that her comfortable world had been irretrievably shattered about three hours ago. Three hours ago she had become a widow.

Of all his jobs, this was the one he loathed the most and which worried him for days afterwards. He went up to the front door and hammered the ornate brass knocker down on to its stud.

The door was opened by a woman with the kind of round, beautiful face that made it difficult to judge her age. Doherty guessed it to be about twenty-five. She had a slim figure with the right curves that were carefully underlined by her clothes.

'Is your mother in?' he asked.

She replied, angrily, that she was Mrs

Rafferty. He cursed himself for having made the same kind of mistake twice in a day. 'I'm Detective Inspector Doherty. May I come in?'

'What...what's happened?' She put her hand up to her heavily lipsticked mouth.

He stepped inside the house and she shut the door. 'I'm afraid there's been an accident,' he said.

'To...to Bill?'

'Yes. In the shooting field.'

'Is he...is he...'

'I'm afraid he's dead.'

'Oh, gawd!' she murmured. She slowly dropped her hand from her mouth.

He heard no sounds other than those of a television set, which suggested she was the only person in the house. Walking stiffly, with eyes focused apparently on some immeasurable distance, she led the way into the sitting-room. There was a cocktail cabinet in one corner and she crossed to it and poured herself out a brandy. She went to one of the leather arm-chairs, sat down, and drank.

He studied her. She was shocked, but almost certainly not as grief-stricken as he would have been had someone suddenly told him that Peggy was dead.

She finished the brandy and when he offered to pour her another, she held out the glass. On his way past the television set he switched it off, cutting short the commentary on an international rugby match.

When she had finished the second drink, she looked up. 'What...what happened?'

'It seems he fell over his gun and it went off.'

'I told him not to go shooting. I begged him not to.' She turned and faced him. 'That sort of thing wasn't for Bill. They'll just laugh at you, I said. Over six hundred quid it cost each of 'em, just to go and shoot something they could buy in the shops at a quid each. Six hundred quid and they never gave Bill more'n a couple to bring back with him. That's all they bloody well gave him, two: can you believe it? Six hundred quid for a couple of birds each time you shoot is plain stupid. I told him. You've paid for 'em all—you tell 'em you want all you shoot. It don't work like that, he said. It's normal only to be given two. D'you know what the matter was? He was scared to ask for more. He went shooting there for just one thing, to be able to talk about going shooting with the Deckers.

I've heard him and the others talking their heads off in the boozer. Good day out shooting, old boy. Been out on the Decker estate. You know the Deckers, don't you? The Deckers of Hurstley Place? Nice folks. Grand old family. Descended from William the Corncurer. Huntin', shootin', and fishin', don't you know.' She began to cry. The tears slid down her cheeks and fell on to her black cashmere. After a few seconds, the tears stopped.

He offered her a cigarette and they both smiled.

'He's dead for sure?' she asked. 'There ain't no chance the hospital can do something for him?'

'I'm afraid not.' He remembered the bloody mess that was part of Rafferty's head.

She looked down at her glass and then across at the cocktail cabinet. He refilled the glass for her.

'How did he get on with the Deckers?' he asked.

She spoke scornfully. 'They was always laughing at him. They knew what he was: their kind can't help knowing. He could pay a thousand quid for a gun and not know the difference, but they knew what he was. I met 'em once: all of 'em. The old woman was dressed in dirty old clothes I wouldn't be seen dead in, but she still knew she was a bleeding sight better than me.'

'Did your husband often see them, apart from a shooting day?'

'Just when he went to pay his cheque, which was the one time they lowered 'emselves enough to have him inside the house. He collected the money from the other three and gave the Deckers something over two and a half thousand quid. All that money just so as they could say they was shooting with the Deckers.'

'Did he ever have a row with any of them?'

'A row? You don't have rows with the likes of them: they just looks through you until you get down and crawl. Bill asked 'em to dinner once, 'though I begged him not to. They thanked him all politely and said they was sorry but was fully booked up and didn't know, like, when they'd be unbooked. Can't stop sticking his neck out, can't Bill. He knows they're no better than he is, but he gets down on hands and knees for them to walk over him. I've shouted at him more'n once. You made all your money by working, I tell him. They got given theirs without doing nothing for it, so who's the better person? He never could see it like that. Only yesterday he says...' She suddenly became silent.

'He said what?'

'Said that now they'd have to have us to dinner and it didn't matter how much they stuck their noses in the air.'

'Why would they have to do that?'

She stubbed out her cigarette. 'He was alive then. He was alive this morning. I cooked his breakfast. Two eggs and four bits of bacon and some mushrooms. Always likes a good breakfast.' She looked at the detective. 'We've only been married three year. That ain't very long, is it?'

Doherty made some conventionally sympathetic reply. Bitter experience had taught him that no one could ever comfort another with mere words: grief was a purely personal thing. In any case, he did not have to know her well to be able to judge that it would not be very long before she was worried more about how much money her late husband had left her than that he was her late husband.

* * * *

Detective Constable Pawley, 31, a red-head without too much of the volatile nature traditionally ascribed to red-heads, knocked on the door of the large detached house which stood next to the church in the village of Yarnley-without. Without what, he wondered?

The door was opened by a large, fat, oily man. 'Mr Abbotts?' asked Pawley.

'Abbotts is the name, lad. Joe Abbotts.'

He was not far short of being tight, thought Pawley. 'I'm Detective Constable Pawley.'

'Come on in. Dreadful shock, you know, knocks all the stuffing out of a man. I had a cigarette with Bill and then went to the stand and when it was all over he was dead.' Abbotts brushed his moustache several times. 'Come on through to the sitting-room and have a drink? There's mostly anything you care to name.'

'I'd rather have coffee, thanks.'

'Coffee,' repeated Abbotts, as they walked through. 'You don't mean coffee. Gin, whisky, brandy, rum, or one of them mucky French drinks: you name it, I've got it.' Once in the sitting-room, Abbotts spoke again. 'Did you see him?'

'No, I didn't.'

'I'm telling you, he was a mess. Most of the head missing and just a mess of blood and God knows what else. Bang and he was dead and there was me, just going on shooting.' He brushed his moustache again. 'What's it to be? A brandy?'

'I'd rather have a coffee.'

'Coffee. You don't want coffee. It'll have to come out of a tin, you know.'

'That's O.K by me.'

Abbotts, looking puzzled, walked over to the door. There, he came to a stop. 'We all had a drink or two at the pub afterwards. We was shocked, and no mistake. Old Bill could be a bit of a...a bit of... It's a shock and that's the truth.' He left.

Pawley looked round the room. It was furnished in a smart, but unemotional way: probably, he thought, Abbotts had gone in to one of the furnishing stores in Avonley or Ashford and told them to do their most expensive best. He noticed one furnishing that must be particular to Abbotts: on the walls hung four framed photographs of different women which were as frank as anything in *Playboy*. Obviously, Abbotts was a great man for the girlies.

Abbotts returned to the room with a tray on which was one cup without a saucer, a bottle of milk, a teaspoon, and some sugar in a plastic container. 'It's my housekeeper's day off so I'm on me own. I've done the best I can for the coffee.'

Whilst Pawley added sugar and milk to the odd-coloured coffee, Abbotts poured himself out a drink. When he went across to the settee, he slumped down on it as if his legs could no longer support his considerable weight.

Pawley sipped the coffee and was relieved to find it tasted better than its appearance had suggested it would.

'You're from the police,' said Abbotts loudly, as if he had just made that discovery.

'That's right.'

'You're on about Bill, of course?'

'Yes.'

'Look, let's have a quick whisper in the ear. Is there something funny about what happened?'

'Funny?'

'You know how I mean. Wasn't it an accident?'

'Why d'you ask?'

'I was just wondering, like.'

'You must have a reason?'

'Me? Of course not. How could I have a reason?'

'Then why think it might not have been an accident?'

'I didn't say it was like that.' Abbotts brushed his moustache vigorously. 'It's just... Well, I just wondered, like.'

Pawley checked a further question he had been going to put and instead asked: 'Whereabouts were you standing when it happened?'

'Me? I was at number five. The birds came over real fast, but I couldn't hit 'em. Too bloody fast for me. Whoosh, and they was out of sight. Julian Decker was pullin' 'em down, though. If I could shoot just half as well as him, I'd be proud, and that's a fact.'

'Did you hear Rafferty shoot at all?'

'I heard shooting, naturally, but there's no saying who it was. When the birds come over like that, it's...' Abbotts gestured with his hands, but seemed unable to find the right words. He swung himself round until he could lean against the arm of the settee and rest his feet on the cushions.

'Are you surprised at the accident?'

'Bill always was a bit careless with his

gun. And did that make Julian Decker spitting mad!'

'How did he get on with the Decker outfit?'

'You don't get on with the likes of them.' Abbotts swung his feet back on to the floor and twisted round. His voice rose. 'They're colder than charity. I like to be friendly with everyone, doesn't matter what they are, but they weren't having any. Asked 'em to drop in for a drink anytime, I did. You'd've thought I was trying to lure 'em here for immoral purposes.'

'Did any of you ever have a row with them?'

'Not flipping likely. Look, mate, a row with them and we'd have been off the shoot as quick as a dose of salts.'

'There are other shoots in Kent.'

'Not owned by the Deckers, there ain't.' Abbotts drained his glass. 'Not that I'm saying it was them that mattered. It was the shooting.'

'Of course.'

'I don't care who I shoot or drink with, provided they're friendly. Bill was different, though. D'you know, I told him, let 'em be. But he wouldn't. Spent all his time aching to be invited there to dinner, with his missus. Ever met his missus?'

'No.'

'I wouldn't mind showing her my etchings and that's straight. When I met her before they was married, I envied him. She's got it all, I'm telling you. You name it, she's got it twice over. She's a lot younger than him, of course and that's what makes him so jealous. Still, if she was my missus, I'd be jealous and no mucking about. I wouldn't let her stroll about the woods with anyone else. Old Bill didn't half get ripe when we teased him about Charlie.'

'Charlie?'

'You know Charlie. Charlie Cranleigh.'

'He ran a course with Mrs Rafferty?'

'Our Charlie would run a course with anything that's got two legs and long hair.' Abbotts sniggered. 'And sometimes I reckon he wouldn't worry how long the hair was.'

'D'you think he really ran a course with her?'

'We all joked about it and Bill got really ripe. No sense of humour.' Abbotts stood up and walked unsteadily across to the cocktail cabinet where he helped himself to another drink.

Pawley looked up at the nearest photograph. He wondered whether Mrs Rafferty looked like that when she was being informal.

CHAPTER 4

Detective Sergeant Orr, recalled to duty from his first Saturday off in two months, drove to Henry Decker's house, just behind Avonley High Street. The district was one of large, cumbersome Victoria houses, each in a fairly large garden. Some had been turned into flats and two were offices. Orr parked his car and crossed the pavement, went up the path to the stone steps and climbed them. He knocked on the front door. It was opened by a woman who regarded him with a disapproval that was automatic.

'Is Mr Decker in, please?'

She said he was and reluctantly showed Orr into a sitting-room which was so clean and tidy that he felt it was almost unsafe to move. After a last look round—to see if anything pinchable was lying about, he thought—she left. Henry Decker came in less than a minute later. He shook hands.

'It's just routine, sir,' said Orr. 'There'll be an inquest and the coroner can be a real B if he reckons the police haven't done their job.'

Henry Decker went across to the blanked-off fireplace and switched on the electric fire in the grate. 'It's damned cold in here. Sorry about that, but we use one of the smaller rooms in winter. He stood with his back to the fire. 'Now, how can I help you?'

'You were out shooting today, sir?'

'I was, thanks to my cousins. They very kindly ask me out during the season. Frankly, if they didn't I wouldn't see much sport. In the last few years the cost of shooting has risen so steeply you've got to be either landed gentry or in big business to be able to afford it.'

'It's like everything else, then, sir. Can you tell me where you were when Mr Rafferty was shot?'

'I was number four gun.'

'Could you see him where he was?'

'Not so much as a hair of his head. The place where we stand is a bit like a jungle: it's a mass of pollard ash and willow, bramble and bracken. Still, the birds go over there better than anywhere else and the dogs seem to manage a good pick-up.'

'Would you know whether you heard him shoot at this place?'

'I've no idea. When the shots are like hail in a hail storm, it's impossible to pick out any particular one and know who fired it.'

'People say he was always pretty careless with his gun?'

Henry Decker moved away from the front of the fire and sat down in one of the arm-chairs. 'Like everything else, times have changed. When I was a lad, gun drill was hammered into us by our elders and betters. If we'd dared point a gun anywhere near anyone, we'd have been slung straight off the shooting field and if we'd been fool enough to say it was safe because it wasn't loaded, we'd have got a sharp clip round the ears to help us on the way. But people like Rafferty come to shooting late in life and never have the drill rammed home. I don't suppose he ever realised that a gun could be just as lethal to a human as to a pheasant: not until it was too late.'

'You're not surprised he shot himself?'

'Frankly, I was always scared I would be on the receiving end of the accident. Julian told him time and again that there were only two safe ways of carrying a gun, but he never learned and you'd see him trotting along with it at the trail. There was even one explosive occasion when he was seen to rest the butt on the ground and to lean on the muzzles.'

'Something like he must have done today?'

'I suppose so.'

'Just for the records, sir, what relation are you to the other Mr Deckers?'

'I'm a cousin of the half blood. Our mutual grandfather married twice, the second time to a Bohemian lady, which clearly caused a flutter in the Decker dovecots. I like my ancestors and relations very much, but they do all suffer a certain streak of inherited puritanism. Family pride is one of those double edged weapons which sometimes cuts the wrong person.'

'How would you say the guns got on together, sir?'

'Is that a tactful way of asking how my cousins suffered the four Mustavabeers? I think you ought to ask the people concerned, Sergeant, don't you?'

Orr briefly smiled. 'In my job, sir, we quickly develop thick skins and I've learned to poke and pry into everybody's business without a blush.'

Henry Decker was silent for some time as he stared at the electric fire. 'There was never any overt unfriendliness,' he finally said.

'Nor, I suppose, was there any friendliness.'

There was no answer.

Orr stood up. 'Thanks very much, sir. Sorry to have bothered you.'

Henry Decker stood up. 'I hope this thing won't get inflated out of all proportion just because it's the Decker family that's involved?'

'It won't be inflated by us, sir.'

'No, of course not. I was thinking of the papers.'

'That's one of the penalties of being who they are.'

'Maybe. The trouble these days are that there are very few balancing advantages.'

'I could maybe think of one or two, sir,' said Orr.

They left the room and Henry Decker led the way to the front door and opened it. On his way to the car, Orr looked up at the sky. It promised rain, with black-bellied clouds chasing one another. Maybe Henry Decker didn't think there were any advantages to being the Deckers of Hurstley Place, but he, Orr, could think of one right away: no work on Saturdays.

★ ★ ★ ★

Julian Decker pushed the ready reckoner to one side and rubbed his eyes. He stared down at the sheets of paper, covered with calculations, on his desk. As far as he could estimate, the new government prices review meant that the farm income would fall by about five hundred pounds a year. That was a serious drop and one which it would be impossible to make up. Outsiders thought the Deckers were rolling in money, but the estate swallowed almost every penny of income: his father had for years neglected things so that now there was always more that needed to be done to buildings or land than ever there was money available. One of the worst features of let land was that the rent was at little more than a pre-war level.

His mother came in. She crossed the

room and stood by the fireplace, above which hung the illuminated address that her husband and she had been given on their marriage: fourteen tenants had the honour to assure Fawcett John deCourcy and Lydia Charlotte Decker of their warm wishes for all happiness and humbly hoped their present of a silver salver would be accepted. Around the walls hung other illuminated addresses, presented to the eldest male Deckers on their twenty-first birthdays and marriages. Probably, there would be no more. Tenants these days rarely had the honour to assure their landlords of anything but a claim for reduced rents, and illuminated addresses cost a great deal of money.

'Are you coming in for coffee, dear?' she said.

He gathered up the papers. 'This latest price review is going to knock us quite hard.'

'I'm sure it is. As Dorothy said to me yesterday, the government thinks we're criminals and ought to be punished. She says they're going to rate agricultural land, but that's impossible. What would happen to the cost of farming? Do come and have your coffee while it's still hot, Julian, and try to stop Fawcett being so gloomy. He's talking as if the world's about to come to an end. It so reminds me of Wagner and his *Götterdämmerung*. It's such nonsense.'

'The world, Wagner, *Götterdämmerung*, Fawcett, or what?'

'You're not to laugh at me, Julian, as I'm not in the mood to be laughed at. I can't think what we're going to have for supper. The Danellis have left absolutely nothing in the larder. I've always said the Italians are an utterly feckless race.'

'How they can put up with working here for what we can afford to pay them, I can't think and I'll bet the store cupboard is bulging with tins.'

'You know I don't like eating food from tins. I was always taught that that's the most slovenly form of cooking.'

'When you were taught cooking, there were always half a dozen cooks around so that there wasn't any need for tins.' Julian stubbed out a cigarette he had left to burn in the ash-tray.

'I do hope Barbara knows how to manage a house, dear?'

'It's only two days since you told me how wonderful she'd be.'

'Is it?' Lydia Decker looked astonished.

'Then it will be all right and she'll manage wonderfully. Now come along and have your coffee and cheer up Fawcett. The pain's bad and that always makes him think of nasty things. If Mr what's-his-name was stupid enough to shoot himself, it really isn't up to Fawcett to worry. Of course, one feels sorry for the children...'

'Rafferty hasn't any.'

'Then things have worked out very well and we can forget the children. Now do come along, Julian.'

He followed her out of the study, through the hall, and into the red withdrawing-room.

* * * *

Doherty drove up to Crispin Corner at 11.30 Sunday morning and waited for a gap in the traffic. When it came, he turned on to the main road. A char-à-banc overtook his car and two children, kneeling on the back seat, pulled faces at him: he stuck out his tongue at them and they became open-mouthed from astonishment.

Fine rain began to fall and he switched on the windscreen wipers. Each time the right-handed one reached the end of its arc, it squeaked and invariably he promised himself he'd get the garage to cure it, but he never remembered. Peggy said he forgot on purpose, so that he could suffer: she claimed the Irish needed to suffer to be able to enjoy life.

He wondered what the pathologist and the gun expert would have to tell him. So far, the whole thing was no more than a series of hints which refused to be pinned down. After a few years, any detective worth his salt developed an instinct where crime was concerned, but if the same detective was utterly frank he would admit that that instinct could be very wrong from time to time. Was his instinct wrong in the present instance when it said that somewhere along the line something was false?

An E-type Jaguar went streaking past the Hillman on a bend, using up the whole of the middle lane and careless about the possibility of another car being in the middle lane. Doherty waited for the harsh and brutal sounds of metal ripping into metal, but there was none. One more driver was escaping his just deserts. Was one of the guns at Hurstley Place hoping to escape his just deserts?

At the by-pass roundabout outside Ashford, Doherty took the second entrance into the town. He followed the road round the World War One tank, now housing electrical transformers, and then, cursing the one-way system drove round the town to the police station. He parked in front of a police 'No Parking' sign. Being in a 'foreign' division, he went into the station and had a word with the duty inspector, an old friend, before leaving and driving on to the morgue.

Rafferty lay on a marble slab in the dissecting room. Doherty stared at the body and thought, as he always did in similar circumstances, how strange a thing was life and death and how little separated one from the other. It was not an original thought, nor was it a cheerful one. He lit a cigarette and morbidly wondered whether the cigarette was hastening him towards his marble slab.

Williams, the gun expert, arrived as the pathologist, dressed in green gown and wearing green rubber gloves, entered the dissecting room. Williams studied the body, had a few quick words with the pathologist, and then asked for the gun. Doherty gave it to him and he went into one of the small rooms to the right.

Half an hour later, the pathologist gave Doherty a plastic bag with a large number of lead pellets in it. Doherty carried them through to Williams, who had divided the gun into its three component parts and then removed the detachable sidelocks.

Doherty put the pellets down on the laboratory bench. Williams looked up. 'There's nothing wrong with the mechanism of this gun. Best quality, regularly checked, with everything in good working order.'

'Was the safety catch working properly, sir?'

'I've just said everything was.' Williams had a brusque manner that often became rude. When he spoke, he clipped many of his words short.

'With the safety catch on the off position, is the gun likely to go off on its own account?'

'If you're fool enough to drop it on the ground, it may go off. If you're a bigger fool and drop it from a bigger height, it may go off even with the safety catch on. The safety mechanism locks the trigger blade and prevents trigger movement: it doesn't prevent the striker falling.'

'Can you suggest how near to his head

the gun was when it went off?'

'It clearly wasn't a contact wound because there's no scorching. Although the angle of the shot means we can't be definite, there doesn't seem to have been any spread of shot: that means under six feet, since it was the right barrel that was fired and this is an improved cylinder boring. Naturally, I'll be conducting various tests with this gun, but it's almost safe to say that tattooing always stops at three feet. As there was some tattooing, I'm prepared at the moment to put the distance at eighteen inches.

'The gun has twenty-five-inch barrels and a short stock. This means that if the dead man rested the butt on the ground and leaned his head forward, his head would be about eighteen inches above the gun. That, of course, is the only conceivable position in which he could have received the wound, if self-inflicted. Was there any depression in the ground to mark the recoil of the butt?'

'No, sir, but the ground was dry and there was quite a bit of dead bracken lying around.'

'The report says he was known to be careless with a gun and someone even saw him once rest the butt on the ground and the muzzles against his stomach. The man was a bloody fool. Well, Inspector, at the moment all I can tell you is that on the face of it, it could have been an accident. He might have been standing upright, with head tilted forward, and he might have dropped the gun when the safety catch was off or have caught the triggers with something.'

'Is there any significance in the fact that the gun was facing outwards and not inwards?'

'The jolt of the recoil might throw the gun over and against its balance so that the muzzles end up pointing away from the body and not, as you'd expect, towards it. I'll have to conduct experiments on that point, of course.'

'Then as far as you can say, sir, it could have been an accident, but if so, it was an odd one?'

'If it was his gun that killed him, yes. One of the alternatives you mustn't overlook is that he was killed when someone else's gun accidentally fired.'

'Wouldn't that other person have come forward?'

'If he were an experienced gun, he might

be too ashamed to admit to being so grossly careless. A first-class shot is a touchy man: I can conceive that a kind of pride might keep him silent.'

'Is there anything to suggest it wasn't murder, sir?'

'Nothing. The muzzle of the weapon that killed the man was about eighteen inches from his head and pointing at an angle of about seventy degrees. Those facts support several possibilities.' Williams picked up the bag of shot and rolled several pieces on to the palm of his hand. Then, he put them down and went to his bag and brought out three pieces of measuring and weighing equipment. For the next ten minutes, he measured and weighed pellets.

'Number five shot, Inspector,' he said. He picked up the used cartridge that had been in the gun and looked down at it. 'The dead man was using five shot. It's a pity some of the charge escaped the body since I can't therefore tell you anything about the bore of the cartridge.'

'Could you have?'

'Different bores use different weights of shot. There's considerable overlapping, but sometimes one can say definitely that only a twelve, sixteen, or twenty bore, fired the shot. Was anyone using anything but a twelve bore?'

'I'm afraid I haven't checked, sir.'

'You should have done so.'

Doherty watched Williams put the three parts of the gun into a leather case on which, stamped in gold, were the initials W.R.

'I'll give you a full report as soon as possible,' said Williams.

'Thank you, sir.' And a fat lot of good it looks as if that's going to be, thought Doherty gloomily.

CHAPTER 5

Doherty parked in front of Hurstley Place, climbed out of the car, and stood in the drive. The drizzle of the morning had turned into rain. In the bad light and the wet the mansion to him looked like a mausoleum.

He went up the steps, between the pillars of the porch, and across the flagstones to the front door. He knocked on the door.

Lydia Decker opened it. 'Good afternoon,' she said.

'Detective Inspector Doherty, madam,' he answered.

'I'm glad to say I both recognised and identified you on sight. My sons, no respectors of age, say that I never remember anyone, but it isn't so. Come in, Mr Doherty, out of this terrible weather. It's the kind of day that makes me feel blue and blue is such a terrible colour. It makes me think of that horrible woman, Clytemnestra. Do you find that?'

'Not quite, no.' He stepped inside.

'But you're Irish, surely?' She closed the door.

'I am, but...'

'I have Irish blood in me and am very proud of the fact. It's my Irish blood which makes me so responsive to colours and I'm surprised you're not the same. How long ago?'

'How long ago what, madam?'

'I simply cannot stand being called madam. It makes me think of brothel keepers.'

Doherty failed to hide his startled surprise.

'Aren't they called madames?'

'Yes.'

'I thought so. They say such people make a great deal of money and, of course, they don't pay any income tax. Income tax is a wicked thing when it's as penal as it is in this country. Do you see that pistol over there?'

Doherty, struggling to keep abreast of the sense of her conversation, looked across the hall at a percussion cap pistol which hung on the wall between two displays of Scottish claymores.

'A Decker wore that in eighteen forty-eight in the Irish uprising following one of the potato famines. He was only an ensign, but when they told him to order a charge on the starving rioters, he refused. His senior officer tried to disgrace him, but in those days if you were a Decker you could twist a few tails. Do you see that duelling pistol a little farther on? That belonged to a Decker who fought a duel and was badly wounded: it's supposed to have given his wife a fatal distemper, but I'm sure women were built of stouter material than that. It's his coat of arms over there: his wife was a Bassett. Heraldry is a fascinating subject and so very frank. You can hardly hush up a family scandal if the shield tells everyone all about it. I'm boring you, Mr Doherty.'

He was so startled by this abrupt change of subject that it was some time before he hastily told her he was not in the least bored.

'I'm an old woman with more memories than I like to admit to. I've always been fascinated by private history and whenever I walk in this house I see the Deckers of all the past centuries. My maiden name was Awcott and the Awcotts are distantly related to the Deckers so that I've always felt that their history is mine. Are you interested in history?'

'It all depends...'

'Last time we met I'm sure you thought that this kind of history and a family who's lived in one place for so long is rather comical?'

'I...er...' said Doherty weakly, unable to find a reply to this accurate description of his feelings.

'This is a very big house and it seems to have become immoral these days to live in a big house. But I don't think we really do anyone any harm by living here. Do you think we do?'

'I'm sure you don't.'

'It's kind of you to say that. But why are we standing here in this draughty hall? Come into the green withdrawing-room: it may be just a little warmer in there. That's the room in which the Decker had a fatal stroke when he learned his wife had been cuckolding him. His ghost is supposed to haunt the room, but I've never seen it. If I did, I'd tell it precisely what I think on the subject. If he couldn't look after her, he was a nincompoop and deserved what happened. He's that mournful man in the painting by the carriage clock in the other room. He has very long hair which makes him look like a... What do they call those long haired boys and girls?'

'Beatniks?'

'That's right.' Lydia Decker led the way into the smaller of the two withdrawing-rooms and as soon as she was inside she pointed to a framed sampler. 'That was done by Amanda Decker at the age of nine. It's quite monstrous and must have ruined her eyes. No wonder she never got married, but gave herself over to good works. When did your family leave Ireland?'

Once again, Doherty had to jerk his mind along to keep up with the change of conversation. 'During the great potato famine. They went to America.'

'Perhaps they were some of the people Peverill Decker refused to slaughter. After all, stranger things have happened. The Decker history is a long one, Mr Doherty, but I'm scared it's not going to last very much longer. My husband thought estates would always last, but I didn't and that's why I persuaded him to give Hurstley Place to a trust in nineteen-fifty-four to escape the death duties which would have ruined it. He died just two days after the five year period was up and because the lawyers had for once done what they were told to, the estate escaped death duties. Just afterwards, of course, the Conservative Government made the five year period less rigid, but I can never remember what they did. Now the estate's in trust for my elder son, provided he reaches thirty-five and accepts it. He's very ill, of course, and that's why the conditions are there. The law is so terribly complicated, isn't it?'

'I'm afraid it is.'

'Can I offer you something to drink, Mr Doherty?'

'No, thank you very much.'

'Julian has worked so very hard to

make the estate pay, but it's terribly difficult. There's always something that needs money spent on it. It's like this house which is forever producing some kind of rot or woodworm. Do you know anything about wood beetles?'

'No, I don't.'

'Julian spends a lot of time squirting nasty smelling stuff into the holes, but they seem to resist rather well. Did you want to speak to my son? He's having luncheon with his fiancée at her house. Miss Harmsworth is a charming girl and I know she'll look after this house most wonderfully.'

'As Mr Julian Decker's away, I wonder if I could have a word with Mr Fawcett Decker?'

'He's not very well today. It's such a horrible illness he suffers from. If only it attacked people's brains as well as their bodies so that they didn't realise what was happening to them. It's an impossible penance to be tied to a wheel-chair and yet to retain an active brain. I've always said that if a person is stupid, he can put up with almost anything.' She looked at her watch. 'I'm very sorry, Mr Doherty, but I must hurry away. It's so nice of you to call and do please come again and tell me more about your ancestors. I feel positive that they were some of the people Peverill Decker refused to kill. If only we had a photograph of the scene we could tell, but I suppose no one had invented photography by then. It's so annoying it took so long. I've always wanted to know what Cleopatra really looked like because I'm sure she wasn't so very beautiful: it's just that men sometimes become so foolish.'

Within ninety seconds, Doherty had been shown out of the house. He walked to his car and was about to open the driving door when he turned and looked up at the house once more: it was still a large, and mainly graceless, conglomeration of bricks and mortar, but now he could see it as a small slice of history. All old houses had housed a succession of people, but the people of this mansion were known. The Deckers could point to a painting and say that that was the Decker who had had his head chopped off in good Queen Bess's day, or had fought against Cromwell and hidden in an oak tree. A man would find importance in himself if he were a Decker, not because of the name or the fortune, but because he was the living example of an endless tradition.

Doherty climbed into the car, started the engine, and drove round the circular lawn and out of the garden into the park. On the right, a tractor was ploughing, turning a stubble field into an ocean of miniature frozen brown waves: on the left, a flock of sheep grazed. He thought, with quick amusement, of how Mrs Decker had not stopped talking whilst he was in the house and, because he had encouraged her, how she had unwittingly answered so many of the questions he had needed answering.

As he slowed down for the road, his mood of self-congratulation suddenly went when he wondered whether she was quite as stupid as he was thinking. He remembered how she had so correctly pin-pointed his previous feeling of light, amused, even sarcastic tolerance for a family like the Deckers. That made him review all she had just told him and, being perfectly self-honest, it soon became rather mortifyingly clear that all she had done was to give him information he could have learned from others and then very neatly bundled him out of the house before he had a chance to ask anyone anything about the shooting.

He brought the car to a halt between

the wrought-iron gates as he waited for an oncoming car to pass. He had not been dealing with a rather foolish, garrulous old woman: he had been dealing with a highly intelligent woman who had taken his measure with no trouble at all.

* * * *

Charles Cranleigh lived in Trisham, a small village half-way between Avonley and Farston in a part of Kent which had somehow escaped the haphazard development that was inundating and ruining so much of the county.

He and his wife had bought a sixteenth century Kentish farmhouse, excellently preserved and almost completely original. Within three years they had destroyed all its charm in the name of modernisation. They did not mix with the villagers, finding them stupid and uncouth. For their part, the villagers found them stupid and uncouth.

Detective Sergeant Orr called at the house at 4.35 on Sunday afternoon. Cranleigh left him in the hall and went through to the sitting-room to speak to his wife. 'It's a policeman come to see me.'

'They've no right to come bothering us

on a Sunday,' she snapped.

'He only wants to ask some questions about yesterday.'

'I don't care what he wants. Well, I'm not having him in here and that's that. If you must speak to him, go into your study, but get rid of him quickly.'

He returned to the hall and showed Orr into the small room at the end of the house. 'You won't be too long, will you? We're just about to have tea.'

Orr rubbed his battered nose, the legacy of several years as an amateur boxer. The mention of tea reminded him how thirsty he was. He waited, but there was no offer of a cup. 'This is just a routine check to see if you can help us any more over yesterday. Whereabouts were you standing?'

'I was at number two stand and it's no lie to say not a single bird came within range of me. I don't mind admitting the shoot costs me over six hundred quid a year and when a bloke pays out that sort of money he expects something back in return.'

Orr had taken an instinctive dislike to this tall, thin, foppishly dressed man and he felt glad the shoot had proved so unprofitable. 'Did you see the dead man at all during the time you were at number two stand?'

'No, of course not.'

'Why do you say of course not?'

'You can't see anyone else. The place is a jungle.'

'And you didn't leave your place?'

'I certainly didn't, no.'

'Just having to check up on everything, Mr Cranleigh. Tell me, would you say that Mr Rafferty was always very careless with his gun?'

'I wouldn't say anything of the sort. Julian Decker was always complaining about it, but you can't keep a gun pointing at the ground all the time. With him, it's anything to find fault. What if Bill did swing his gun round a bit?'

'Then things must have got a bit dangerous from time to time?'

'He kept the safety catch on mostly. Anyway, as often as not the gun wasn't even loaded.'

'What size shot were you using?'

'What size shot? What's that to do with the police?'

'It's part of the inquiries, sir.'

'What I use, or don't use, hasn't anything to do with the inquiries. He shot himself and that's an end to it.'

'Are you refusing to say?'

'What d'you mean, refusing? Certainly not.'

'I thought you were.'

'Not in the sense you're trying to make out. I know my rights, Sergeant, and I...'

'What size shot were you using?'

'Well... It was number five. Julian Decker always uses number five for pheasants or driven duck.'

Orr wrote in his note-book.

'What are you putting that down for?' demanded Cranleigh.

'As I said earlier, we just have to check.' Orr looked up. 'Were you pretty friendly with Mrs Rafferty?'

Cranleigh stared with sudden consternation and fear at the detective. He turned and quickly looked at the door as if he expected his wife to come into the study. 'That...that's a lie.'

'Then you don't know her at all?'

'Of course I know her. But I'm not friendly with her like you've just said. You've no right to come here and make those dirty insinuations...'

'I haven't insinuated anything.'

'You were deliberately suggesting that...

that there was something...'

'Is there?'

'I'll complain to the chief constable about this. By God, I will. He's a personal friend of mine: d'you know that?'

'He's a very friendly man, but he issued an order a year ago that when it came to work the force was to understand that he didn't have any friends.'

'Well I...I know him very well.' Cranleigh, realising how weak his threat now sounded, became defensive in manner. 'Look, it's not nice of you to come here and suggest that sort of thing.'

Orr thought of the other as a self-inflating balloon which deflated at the slightest prick. 'I gather one or two people have joked with you about it. Is that right?'

'I'm happily married. My wife's in the other room. You can't...you can't say that sort of thing.' Cranleigh slowly sat down.

'They do say that where there's smoke there's fire?'

Cranleigh took a handkerchief from the top pocket of his blazer, on which was a large gold crest, and mopped his forehead. 'There's nothing to it: nothing at all.'

'Are you quite certain?'

'Look, I may have had a little joke, but honest to God that's the beginning and end of it. Just because I've joked about knowing Daphne, that doesn't mean...mean anything. It was only that... Look, I'm very happily married and I wouldn't mess around with another woman. If you're married, you'll understand that?'

'I'm married, but I've never joked about going a course with another woman.'

Cranleigh suddenly stood up. 'Who's been on to you about this? Who's been spreading these rumours?'

Orr merely shrugged his shoulders.

'I suppose it was one of the others. That's the kind of thing they'd do.' Cranleigh lit a cigarette with hands that trembled. 'All right, if you're so busy prying you find out about Phil Wade. Him and Bill Rafferty like each other like cat and dog: you ask Phil about the way he was losing control of his business. That ought to give you something concrete to check up on.'

'We'll certainly look into the matter.'

There was a pause. 'You won't tell him I've said anything, will you?' pleaded Cranleigh.

You poor wet bastard, thought Orr.

★ ★ ★ ★

Doherty interviewed Wade on the Monday morning, in the latter's office in Ferry Road. Doherty was shown into the large, luxuriously furnished office by an ugly woman of uncertain age. Wade came round his desk and shook hands and once again Doherty was struck by the almost unblinking stare of the other's pale-blue eyes: reptilian, was the description that occurred to him.

'This is an expected pleasure,' said Wade, in his soft voice.

'Expected?'

'I've heard the police are making inquiries so it was reasonable to assume you would be along to see me. I presume that the shooting wasn't just a straightforward accident?'

'We don't yet know, sir.'

'Or are you not yet committing yourselves? No matter, we expect the police to be the silent service. Sit down, Inspector. You'll find that the red chair is fairly comfortable.'

Doherty sat down in the heavy leather arm-chair.

'A cigarette? Or are you a member of the small, but no doubt healthy, minority who eschew the vice?'

'I'd like one very much, thanks.'

Wade proffered a gold cigarette case. He spoke again as he flicked open a gold lighter and gave Doherty a light. 'What would you like to know?'

'A check up on where you were standing at King's Beat and what size shot you were using.'

'I was number one gun, which entailed walking down with the beaters to the cross-ride and then hurrying down behind the other guns to the stand. Some time ago I queried why it was not number seven gun who came down with the beaters, so saving the final extra walk, but Julian Decker made the not inconsiderable point that the birds which break forward early almost invariably go over number seven so that there must be a gun there from the beginning. Very few birds ever seem to go over number one.'

'What size shot were you using?'

'What's the significance of that?'

'Just a matter of routine, sir.'

'An unnecessary routine if it was an accident.'

'I haven't suggested it was anything else.' Doherty watched the other smile briefly and thought he had never seen an expression of less humour.

'Inspector, this world is run by what isn't said. If Bill died from a straight accident, you couldn't possibly be interested in the size of shot I use.'

Doherty said nothing.

'What are the possibilities? I suppose the accident at the hands of someone else, or murder. Did someone kill him in cold blood? I'd say that's highly likely. He was an unlikeable man who'd been very successful: success naturally breeds dislike so that he was doubly unpopular.'

'I'm told you know something about his business successes?'

'Are you?'

'Wasn't he gaining control of your business?'

Wade became motionless except for his right hand, resting on top of the desk, which clenched and unclenched.

'Is it true you were in business conflict with him?'

'Who's been shouting from the roof-tops?' Wade spoke harshly. Then, with great self-control, he reverted to his previous light sarcasm. 'One of the other two, of course, and my old pal Charlie as first guess. The poor man's Casanova. The sexual athlete, or the five women miler.'

'We're already checking on a point or two there, sir.'

'Good. Then I needn't drop any more hints.'

'As shooting partners, you seem to have had your differences?'

'It was our dislike of each other that kept us together. Hatred is the most binding of human emotions.'

'Then you hated Rafferty?'

Wade leaned back in his chair. 'I am a clever businessman, but now that he is dead and out of the way I'll admit that Bill Rafferty was just fractionally more clever: perhaps it was because he did not underrate me, but I assessed him at his true worth. My business was about to fall into his hands at considerable loss to me.'

'You certainly had reason to hate him, then?'

'Shall we say that I had no cause to love him. I want to make it clear that my dislike would never have prodded me into physical action. I'm very strong on words, but very weak on action.'

'There's little action attached to the pulling of the trigger of a shotgun.'

'But think of the violent mental action necessary.'

'Now he's dead, what'll happen to your business?'

'I'll save it. Joe Abbotts, Rafferty's business associate, whipping boy, yes man, and clown, is essentially a fool. I shall be all right.'

'Rafferty's death can be called providential for you?'

'Exceedingly. To such an extent it shakes my faith as an atheist.'

Doherty stubbed out the cigarette. He studied Wade's face. 'You haven't said what size shot you use?'

'Six and a half. When it was brought out a few years ago it seemed to me a sensible compromise. In any case, I am reluctant to use the same as Julian Decker and, as a direct consequence, all the others. Had he stood on his head to shoot, they would have endeavoured to do the same.'

'Why shoot at Hurstley Place if you disliked everyone so much?'

'I've already said, it was our mutual dislike which formed the bond. In any case, it's the best shoot in this part of Kent.'

'There's one last question, Mr Wade. When you walked down the ride behind the other guns, did you see anyone?'

'Miss Harmsworth went into the Larch Plantation with her dog to pick-up. And, of course, before that there was the beater who was on the top ride as a stop.'

'But no one else?'

'No one. And let me assure you that had I seen anyone I'd have absolutely no hesitation in telling you.'

Doherty stood up. 'Thank you.'

'Inspector?'

'Yes?'

'If you're searching for a motive, have a think about Bill and the Deckers.'

'What do you mean exactly?'

Wade's eyelids seemed to close slightly. 'I'm surprised no one's mentioned it?'

'When I know what you're talking about, I'll know if anyone's spoken.'

'Bill was the complete and utter snob, an infliction that strikes undeveloped intellects. He had one social ambition in life: to be asked with his wife to dine with the Deckers. The fact that this was one of the most unlikely events of the century merely spurred on his ridiculous ambition. On Saturday, he was boasting that the Deckers were going to have to receive him and his wife. He was even willing to bet on it.'

'I see.'

'You consider that of no account?'

'I can't possibly say at the moment.'

Wade began to tap on the desk with his fingers.

'Thanks for your help,' said Doherty. He walked across to the door.

'What size shot did you say killed him?' asked Wade.

'I didn't,' replied Doherty, as he opened the door.

CHAPTER 6

On Tuesday morning it rained in a steady and sullen downpour. At Hurstley Place, the lights in the dining-room were switched on to enable the family to see to eat their breakfast.

'Bloody weather,' muttered Fawcett. He turned round in his wheel-chair and stared out of the nearest full-length window.

'Rain always makes me feel sad,' said Lydia Decker. 'As a little girl, whenever it rained I used to go and hide under the billiards table...'

'The last time you told the story it was the cupboard under the stairs,' interrupted Fawcett.

'Was it, dear? Well, I know it was one or the other. There's not really very much difference, is there, when you think that it was the rain which caused it all.'

Julian pushed the letters and bills which had arrived by the morning post to the side of his place at the huge table at which they sat: it would seat twenty-four people in elbow comfort and he frequently suggested they should use a much smaller one, but his mother always found some objection to this. He studied Fawcett. His brother was still in one of his black moods which meant that the rest of them had to exercise all the patience they could muster.

'I think I'll go and live somewhere sunny like the south of Spain,' said Lydia.

'You know wild horses wouldn't drag you away from this place,' said Fawcett.

'I shall be moving to the dower house when Julian marries.'

'You'll still be physically close to here. This damned estate has become a set of shackles around each of us. If we sold up now with the price of land it is, we'd get half a million for it which would give an income of twenty-five thousand. We could get abroad and begin to live. Instead of which, we stay on here in a house twenty times too big for us and worry year in and year out because we've hardly enough income to buy collar studs.'

Julian stood up and crossed to one of the serving tables. He poured himself out another cupful of coffee. 'With the politics as they are, it's better to have money tied up in land than lying around loose as capital.'

'I'm not talking about keeping the money in this country so that those communist bastards in parliament can pinch it. Get the money out: go and live in the Bahamas: forget you're a Decker and your land was enfeoffed to the Lanchvilles soon after William the Conqueror was around. You don't think this country wants to have anything more to do with you? We're the filthy rich: we live on the life-blood of our tenants who pay us a rent that was barely economic before the war.' Fawcett turned the wheel-chair round and hurried it across the floor to the nearest door. He pushed the door open and went out.

Back in the dining-room, they could hear swish of the rubber tyres and a squeak that occurred once every turn of the wheels.

'Oh, dear,' sighed Lydia. 'He's very ill again. It all seems so hopeless, Julian. When he started becoming ill your father and I took him to many specialists in this country and even to two in Berlin, but it was no good. He surely doesn't really think we should sell Hurstley?'

'Of course not.'

'You seem to know him so much better than I do these days. He couldn't really mean that, could he? It's a kind of trust for all the generations. Your children will have children and they'll inherit the estate and pass it on to their children. Sometimes, it makes me think it explains a little of what life's about. I used to say that to your father and he'd laugh. He said that only those who had nothing proved the continuity of existence since they passed on all they possessed. At least, I think that's what he said. D'you think it makes sense?'

Julian went back to his chair, one of a set of eighteen Hepplewhites, and sat down. 'It probably does.'

'Julian, you're distrait. Has there been bad news in the post? I've always hated the post. People ought to have the decency not to write bad news as breakfast certainly isn't the time to receive it.'

'There are just the usual crop of bills. The estimate for the roof of the wing is fifteen hundred, so it'll have to wait.'

'It can't wait or the weather will ruin the timber. I shall pay for it.'

'Mother, your money...'

'Is my money and I can spend it how I want. The only use of money is to spend it, your dear father always used to say. I remember his telling that to a bank manager when he was obtaining some sort of overdraft. The bank manager was a very earnest man and he tried to suggest your father carried on his financial affairs differently. I'm sure he was only trying to help, but it so annoyed your father that he went straight out and lost a hundred pounds on the Two Thousand Guineas. Or was it the Oaks? I don't remember. What's Fawcett worrying about?'

Julian buttered another piece of toast

and helped himself to more marmalade. 'I'm afraid I've no idea.'

'I'm sure you really do know and are just refusing to tell me. Is it about that terrible accident?'

'I just don't know, Mother.'

'Fawcett mustn't worry so. Everything's going to be all right. I had a premonition and my premonitions are never wrong.'

Julian forbade to remind her of her last expressed premonition which had been on the same subject and totally unfavourable. He loved his mother, particularly for her apparent eccentricity. So many of her contemporaries believed it to be their duty to conform to the picture they ought to present to the world, but she didn't give a damn for the world.

'Have you heard any more?' she asked.

'About what?'

'You know very well what I'm referring to.'

'Your premonitions?'

'Julian, you're getting more and more obstructive. I want to know whether anything more has happened about that horrible man's death? Has that pleasant policeman been asking you a lot of questions?'

'Which pleasant policeman?'
'The Irish one.'
'I haven't seen him.'
'Are you sure?'
'Cut my throat and hope to die.'

The far door of the dining-room, leading into the butler's pantry, opened and Danelli came in. He and his wife were the only servants in the house and from the way in which they seemed not to care how hard they worked it could easily have been mistakenly thought that they had been with the family for many, many years. 'Anything more?' asked Danelli, his voice thick with accent.

Lydia turned. 'No more, thank you. Tell your wife we are having the joint for lunch.'

'You are having cold meat.'

'I told her quite specifically that we were having the joint today with roast potatoes and those frozen peas which don't taste quite as awful as the others. It's a nice big joint of beef...'

'Yesterday.'

'We had the beef yesterday? Did we? Yesterday was Monday and we had...'

Julian, having finished his breakfast, collected up his mail and left. He went through to the hall and the office beyond.

He lit a cigarette, crossed to the window, and looked at the wing. It consisted of a very large ballroom and some very small bedrooms above. His mother was going to spend a great deal of money on repairing the roof and when she died he was going to pull the wing down so that her money would be wasted. But he couldn't tell her that. If she knew he was going to pull the wing down, she'd return after death to haunt him day in and day out. To her, every last brick was sacred, to be religiously preserved, no matter when it dated from.

He was presuming Hurstley Place would still belong to the family when she died. It was a dangerous presumption. Rafferty had threatened to hurt the Deckers as hard as he could, perhaps even mortally, and now the question must be whether he would reach from beyond the grave to carry out his threat. If it happened like that, the estate would be destroyed. Not even his, Julian's, mother could prevent that.

He turned away from the window and looked up at the stags' heads on the wall above the illuminated addresses. Most of them had been shot in Scotland by his grandfather. In his grandfather's day both the Decker family and Hurstley Place were destined to go on forever.

Had Rafferty suffered an accident, as it always seemed he must because of the utterly careless way in which he handled his gun? Or had someone shot him by accident and was now too scared to speak up? Or had someone murdered him?

Julian left the office and went through the hall to the gun-room where he changed into wellingtons. In the glass-fronted cabinet on the wall were the Decker guns. A .475 double-barrel rifle, a 6.5 mm. magazine rifle, a couple of .22 rifles, a 3" chambers 12 bore, a best pair of Holland and Holland 16 bore, a pair of ancient but beautiful Holland and Holland hammer 12 bore, a hammerless non-ejector 28 bore, two double and one single .410c, and a garden gun. When a Decker learned to shoot, he started at the bottom with an empty garden gun and slowly worked his way up. He carried the garden gun for months before he was allowed to fire it: then he graduated to one of the .410s, changed to the 28 bore, and finally was granted the supreme honour of one of the 16 bore Holland and Holland. Two or three years ago, he and Fawcett had thought about changing the pair of 16s for a pair of 12s, but the cost had been too great and the advantage gained doubtful.

Julian slowly put on a coat of thornproof material. What evidence had Rafferty left lying about for the police to discover and uncover? How much did his tame fat shadow, Abbotts, know?

Julian stubbed out the cigarette. He was having lunch with Barbara. Her father was a merchant banker and the newspapers always referred to him as a millionaire and quoted the length of his cigars. He wasn't in the Getty class, but he was wealthy and eventually his money would come to Barbara, who in any case had a small fortune in her own right, left to her by an aunt. Julian first met her at a birthday party, meant to launch the daughter of the house into the world of society: the daughter had been living with some sort of weirdie in outer Chelsea and hadn't wanted to be launched anywhere. He had been about to leave, only half an hour after arrival, when he saw Barbara, dancing with a man with a beard. He had brashly claimed a previous acquaintance and then he had gone on to surplant the man with the beard. It was unshakably right that a Decker should marry a girl with money because Hurstley Place needed money as the earth needed rain to make it fruitful. He hadn't proposed to her because she was wealthy, but her wealth had been no hindrance.

He picked up a hat and prepared to go into the lashing rain. Still, his mind kept asking questions. Suppose Rafferty had left behind enough proof for the police to discover the truth—how would, he Julian, be affected? He supposed he had committed some sort of a crime. Would they try him for it and perhaps imprison him? Could it possibly affect Barbara and him? He angrily told himself that that was a ridiculous question. Barbara was not the kind of person to retire at the first hint of trouble: on the contrary, she was more likely to roll up her sleeves and go out to meet trouble half-way.

★ ★ ★ ★

Detective Superintendent Quincy, in charge of the county's C.I.D, and Doherty understood each other's faults, which made for a pleasant relationship. In many ways, they complemented each other: the superintendent was normally pessimistic but had a round, roly-poly face that suggested a happy disposition, whereas Doherty was normally optimistic but his face, when in repose, looked so gloomy that it seemed as if he must just have committed suicide.

Quincy sat on the edge of Doherty's office desk and swung his right leg backwards and forwards. 'Well, Sam?'

'That just about sums everything up, sir.'

'What's to do?'

'Not much, and that's a fact. It's like a play by Pirandello: five characters with motives in search of a murder.' Doherty went round his desk and sat down. He opened the top right-hand drawer and brought out a small tin of whiffs. 'D'you use these?'

'With the price of tobacco what it is, I use anything that's offered.' He accepted one of the whiffs. 'How d'you make five?'

Once his cigar was alight, Doherty leaned back in his chair. The two Deckers...'

'Hell, man, you told me that one of 'em's permanently in a wheel-chair.'

'If you saw him manoeuvre the thing around you wouldn't cross him off any list just because of that. The two Deckers were under some sort of pressure from Rafferty. Then there's Cranleigh who may have mucked around with Rafferty's wife a bit more heartily than he's so far admitted, and Wade who was on the wrong end of Rafferty's business dealings.'

'All right, that's four. Who's number five?'

'Mrs Decker.'

'Who? For God's sake, Sam, how can you say something like that? Have you been on the marijuana?'

'She loves that house and estate like you and I love our wives. If it was really threatened, she'd do anything in the world to save it, and damn the consequences. I've checked. She was supposed to be in the house at the time, but she could easily have been at King's Beat.'

'But Mrs Decker...' Quincy got off the desk, crossed the floor, and looked at the map of the division which hung on the wall. He returned to the nearer chair in front of the desk. 'I knew this case was going to stink. So you've some suspects. Suspects for what? An accident? A murder?'

'I know, sir. That's the question.'

'You're bad for my blood pressure, Sam.

You realise that, don't you? You turn up with a case and don't even damn' well know if it is a case. There must be some evidence somewhere. Is any more forensic evidence in, or something from the gun expert?'

'Nothing.'

'What size shot were they using?'

'All were using five except Henry Decker and Wade.'

'That doesn't really tell you anything, does it?'

'No, sir. If you were going to commit murder, you'd make certain you had one cartridge of the right sort with you.'

'So help me, Sam, I could strangle you. What in the name of hell do I tell the A.C.C? One of my D.I's, sir, is investigating a crime which may very well not be a crime, but he's investigating really hard just the same.'

'You could always say I'm suffering from a hunch.'

'If you're working on a hunch, lose it.'

'Something along the line smells.'

'And I could tell you what, only I've been brought up polite.'

'I'll swear it wasn't a self-inflicted accident.'

'You can swear all you like, but it could have been. That's the evidence.'

Doherty sighed.

'You Irish are all the same: always causing trouble. God knows why we hesitated so long to hand Ireland back to you.' Quincy scratched the back of his round head. 'What's your next move?'

'I'll keep on digging, sir. I want to know what Rafferty was talking about when he said he'd force the Deckers to receive him and his wife. I want to know why Abbotts thought the death wasn't an accident.'

'Did he say he didn't?'

'No. But Detective Constable Pawley saw him and reports that reaction.'

'Pawley. Pawley. Isn't that the red-head who created trouble in Y division when he got on the wrong side of one of the town councillors?'

'I believe something did happen.'

'Well you make certain something doesn't happen here with him.' Quincy stood up and pushed back the chair. 'It's your case, Sam, and I'll make no secret of the fact that I'm leaving you with it so that you can sweat all the blood.' Ash fell from his cigar on to his coat and then on to his trousers. He brushed it off. 'Don't forget for one second you're dealing with the Deckers. Get on the wrong side of them, Sam, and your remaining career with the police is past history: nothing more.'

CHAPTER 7

Barbara and her father lived in a large, handsome Georgian house to the south of Ashford. He had no instinctive love of the country and thought of it merely as offering him a convenient way of living out of London, but she was different and it had been she who persuaded him to buy the farm next to their house when it came up for sale some years previously. Since he had bought the land at seventy-five pounds an acre and it was now worth around two hundred, he thought of the purchase as a reasonably successful one: she knew that this was farm land which would not be built over.

Barbara and Julian had lunch in the dining-room. In front of the larger radiator, Toby, the G.S.P, lay sound asleep but making short yapping noises as he chased after runners in his dreams.

Julian studied Barbara as he ate the grapefruit the housekeeper had served. One of his friends had said that if she put on a bargee's outfit, she would still look like a Dior mannequin: he disliked mannequins, but thought the comparison reasonably apt. Even picking-up, when covered by floppy weatherproof and thornproof clothing, she remained reasonably shapely. She had a softly-featured, regular face with a nose that had a jocular hint of a turned-up tip. Her eyes were round and deep-blue and they contrasted vividly with her black, naturally wavy, hair.

'What are you thinking, Julian?'

He smiled. 'I was assessing your physical features.'

'I thought you were looking averagely lecherous.'

'I told you some time ago that I have a passionate nature.'

'You did, my darling, and by then it was not news.' She pressed the bell-punch under the table and the housekeeper came in, took away the dirty plates, and put on the table clean plates and the dishes of the main course. Toby had woken up and he went up to the housekeeper and smelled her fingers to see if she had any food for him.

'You don't get anything at meal times,' said Barbara sharply.

Toby wagged his truncated tail. It was possible to suppose from his expression that he knew that when his mistress was not looking, he did get something during meal times. When the housekeeper left, he left with her, tail wagging more quickly than before.

Barbara helped herself to fried potatoes and peas. 'Is it a bit cold in here, Julian?'

'Cold. I'd have called it semi-tropical.'

'I'm sure the thermostat's been altered.'

'Mother said the other day that she couldn't think how you'd exist at Hurstley because of the cold. She recommended long woollen underwear. I said it didn't sound like you.'

'Maybe we can install central heating?'

'Maybe,' he replied, his voice suddenly flat.

'Surely we could do it in some of the rooms. There'd be no need to do it in all.'

'I suppose so.'

She looked at him. 'What's wrong, Julian?'

'Wrong?'

'You've been as miserable as anything for some of the time, staring into space and looking like death warmed up.'

He cut a kidney in half.

'Is it this horrible accident that's worrying you?'

He was going to deny that anything was worrying him, but realised the futility of this. 'In a way it is.'

'In what way?'

'It's pretty certain the police don't reckon it was a straightforward accident.'

'Do they think he was deliberately shot?'

'Possibly.'

'Murdered? Isn't that absurd? He was a rather horrible little man, but no one would have deliberately shot him.'

He shrugged his shoulders.

'Well, why should anyone?' she persisted.

'I don't know.' He lacked the courage to tell her what Rafferty had been threatening to do.

'There you are, then. In the end it'll turn out to have been just a nasty accident. Did I tell you a detective had been to see me this morning?'

'No?'

'He was a young man with flaming red

hair. I thought he was a bit brash, but he was perfectly pleasant.'

'What did he want?'

'To ask me where I was during the drive at King's Beat and if I'd seen anyone moving around. I told him I'd seen Wade, but no one else. Wade always makes me think of a stoat. I'm sure he's dangerous.'

'Dangerous?'

'I mean, if you make an enemy of him. He's the only one of the four with any manners, but I'm convinced that underneath them they're all mockery.'

Julian cut a slice off the steak. 'Did the detective ask any other questions?'

'Not really, except he wanted to know how the people of the shoot mixed together. I just said that as far as I knew they all got on well together.'

'That was quite a lie.'

'I wasn't going to tell him anything else.'

'I suppose not.'

She put down her knife and fork. When she spoke, her voice expressed her worry. 'Julian, you're fencing with me.'

'No I'm not.'

'You're terribly worried about something, but you're trying unsuccessfully to hide the fact. What are you afraid of?'

'Nothing.'

'Please tell me.'

'There's nothing to tell you.'

She was silent. Just how serious were things?

* * * *

Doherty parked in the main car-park in Ashford. He walked down to Stanhay where he bought a replacement length of plastic feed-line for his motor-mower, looked at the record-players in Burnage and sighed because he could not afford even the cheapest, then returned to his car. He drove to Station Road, was temporarily held up by a flood of cyclists coming from the railway works, but thereafter had a clear run along Beaver Road.

As he drove, he wondered whether his coming interview with Abbotts was going to get him any further? And if it did, any further in which direction? Had there been an accident or a murder? Would it prove to be a perfect murder because no one was going to be able to prove it to be what it was? Statistics could never say how many perfect murders were committed each year because by their very definition they were deaths about which no one was a hundred per cent sure. The easiest, perhaps the only, way to commit a perfect murder was to mask it as an accident.

The car reached the countryside and once clear of the Tenterden road drove through the twisting lanes that owed nothing to the age of the internal combustion engine. Doherty always enjoyed a sense of contentment when in the country and he could now imagine how the Deckers felt when they stood outside the mansion and surveyed the acres around them and knew those acres were theirs. Land was something you could see, feel, and walk over, and no one could steal it from you—except, of course, the government. He had wanted to be a farmer, but his parents had dissuaded him. What about the potato famines, they had said, as if it had been they who had lived through them and not their ancestors.

If you had a deep love of the land, inherited from generations of land owners, and your land was threatened, you might kill to save it. Equally, if you'd spent your lifetime working up your business and that business was threatened, you might kill to save it. Equally, if you'd been mucking around with a man's wife and he found out about it you might kill to save yourself and get the woman.

The car passed the village signpost of Yarnley-without, on which was set the white horse of Kent. Yarnley-without. When he retired, he wanted to live in a village called by a name like that. It took one back to a world at which time was a plentiful commodity.

He drove past the general store and the public house and reached the cross-roads. Although it was his right of way, a car came in from his left and crossed over. Just one of the perils of living in Yarnley-without. He parked in front of the large house next to the square steepled church, went up the garden path, and knocked on the front door. It was opened by a woman of about thirty who was wearing a silk dress that he guessed had cost a considerable amount of money. She said that Mr Abbotts was in the sitting-room. Obviously, she was the housekeeper: obviously spelt with a capital H.

Abbotts was wearing a country suit in an over-large, bright green check which made him appear very corpulent. 'Nice to see you,' he boomed. 'What'll you drink?'

'I wouldn't mind a beer, thanks.'

'How about something stronger. You name it, I've got it.'

'I usually stick to beer, thanks.'

'Good for the kidneys, eh? Keep 'em flushed and you keep young, as my doctor used to say.'

Abbotts left the room. Doherty stared at the framed photographs of the naked young ladies. They were attractive and seductive, but unreal because who in life had the chance of meeting such charm? Abbotts returned and handed the D.I a silver tankard filled with a pint of beer. Abbotts sat down and lifted his glass of whisky.

'Here's cheers. First today and doubly welcome. Never drink until the sun's over the yard-arm, unless it's business. Then it's a duty.' He chuckled.

Doherty drank slowly. Pawley had contemptuously referred to Abbotts as a windbag, which was an obvious but nevertheless accurate description of the man. In ten years' time, his slack features and body would become gross.

Abbotts waited for the detective to explain the purpose of the visit, but when he remained silent, Abbotts became uneasy. He twice began to speak, then finally said: 'Did you want to ask me something?'

'Yes.'

There was a pause. 'What?' asked Abbotts.

'I want to know what the truth is.'

'Look here, I don't know what you mean. I told the truth to the last bloke who came here asking questions.'

'Did you explain why you thought it might not have been a straightforward shooting accident?'

'But...but I never thought that.'

Doherty ignored the denial. 'Everything suggested it was an accident?'

'Yes, of course.'

'Yet you asked my detective constable whether it was one.'

'Did I? I don't think I did.'

'The only possible reason for asking is that you know some reason why it mightn't have been one.'

Abbotts mopped his forehead with a handkerchief. He finished his drink and stood up, obviously to get himself another.

'What is it?'

Slowly, Abbotts sat down. 'I don't know anything.'

'You've worked with Rafferty for some years?'

'That doesn't mean he told me everything that was going on.'

'But he did in this case.'

'I don't know anything.'

'Why do you think Rafferty was murdered?'

'I don't know.'

'What could the motive be?'

'I don't know.'

'What's got you scared, Mr Abbotts?'

'Scared? Me?'

'You're scared to tell me the truth.'

'I don't know anything.'

Doherty looked at this man who, in so short a time, had had his emotions changed from self-satisfaction to fear. Fear of what?

Doherty drank his beer. When the tankard was empty, Abbotts offered him the other half and became wildly insistent when he refused.

Doherty stood up. 'You won't help us, then?'

'There's no way I can,' mumbled Abbotts.

Doherty left the room. When he reached the front door, the housekeeper came into the hall from the room on the left. 'Good afternoon,' she said, and there was a trace of mockery in her voice.

★ ★ ★ ★

Doherty drove to Hurstley Place on Wednesday morning and after two false calls he found the headkeeper's cottage. He spoke to Mrs Adams, who told him her husband was out repairing the draught-wall in Bourne Shaw where the wind cut through the shaw like a raging tornado.

Following her directions, he drove down the lane, took the first turning on the right, and parked at the point where the land went round to the left. He looked down at his shoes and cursed because he had forgotten to bring any wellingtons: he wondered what Peggy would say when he got back home with shoes caked in mud? Then, he climbed over the wooden gate and began to cross the stubble field. Half-way to the woods, a covey of partridges rose in front of him with a suddenness that startled him. Standing still, he watched them fly round to the right, skim the blackthorn hedge, and pitch down into a field of kale. When he resumed walking, he looked straight ahead and saw a man had stepped out from the trees and was watching him. Almost at once, he recognised Adams.

'Reckoned I'd maybe caught a poacher,' said Adams, when Doherty caught up to him.

'I couldn't hit 'em if they sat and looked at me.'

'The real poachers never worry about guns: it's raisins and fish hooks, or a bantam cockerel with steel spurs.'

Doherty looked past the keeper and saw that just inside the trees there was a wall of straw bales, six feet high. Evidently, draughts were as inimical to pheasants as humans. 'I'd like to have a look round the other beat if it's possible?'

'King's Beat? We can go round there by the Land-Rover.' Adams spoke thoughtfully. 'They're saying Mr Rafferty wasn't such a bloody fool as to blow his own head off?'

'Then they know more about it than I do.'

'It's like that, is it?'

'In a way. But suppose you were told it wasn't an accident, have you any ideas who might have pulled the trigger?'

'I ain't so much as a single thought.'

'Rafferty didn't get on well with the Deckers, did he?'

'I wouldn't know.'

Doherty had expected no other answer. Even if Adams had seen one of the Deckers kill Rafferty, he might well refuse to say so.

They climbed into the Land-Rover and Adams drove round the south end of the shaw and across two fields to a wooden gate in the corner of the woods. Beyond the gate, a ride went both south and north through the trees.

Adams climbed down and slammed the door shut. 'Are you looking for something particular?'

'Just looking,' replied Doherty. 'Will you take me to each stand in turn?'

After half an hour, Doherty was satisfied that any of the guns could have moved through the undergrowth and between the pollard trees without being seen: also, by coming down the ride and up the beaten track to the stand, Fawcett Decker could have reached Rafferty equally unseen.

They were on their way back to the Land-Rover when they met Julian Decker, as he walked down the ride.

'What are you doing here?' demanded Julian.

'Just checking up on a thing or two, sir,' replied Doherty.

Julian spoke to Adams. 'I thought you were going to repair that draught-wall?'

Adams, without a word, turned and walked up the ride.

'Checking up on what?' snapped Julian.

'Whether someone could have pushed through all this undergrowth without being seen and whether a wheel-chair...' He stopped.

'What?'

'Whether a wheel-chair could have gone unseen from the ride to the stand.'

'Get off this land.'

'Very well, sir.' Doherty turned and walked up the ride.

CHAPTER 8

Saturday, November the 20th, was a day of biting east winds and an overcast and dirty sky which promised rain or snow. Avonley, a market town which so far had escaped the Philistine hands of the planners and the new town builders, was normally fairly busy on a Saturday in winter, but on this depressing day the pedestrians were few. Shop-keepers faced empty shops, the policemen on patrol or point duty huddled inside their raincoats, and even Lord Kitchener, a stone figure astride a stone horse, looked miserable and cold.

Avonley police station was old, ugly and had been scheduled for demolition for eight years. The new station would have been built if only the mayor and his corporation had not been quite so obsessed with the more obvious trappings of civic pride. Doherty's room was at the back of the ground floor and as it projected beyond the line of the main block, it stood four square to most of the winds that blew. Most winds which blew seemed to reach inside the room and the electric fire did little to dispel the cold.

Detective Superintendent Quincy stood as close to the fire as he could get. 'It's bloody cold enough to freeze the brass monkey as well.'

Doherty leaned back in his chair. 'One seems to get used to it after a while.'

'I've no intention of trying. Sam, I spent the night down at Tenterden and I reckoned I'd better call in here on my way back to HQ. It seems like it's a long time since I've had a progress report from you.'

'On the shooting, sir?'

'Now listen, man, it's not some farthing pick-pocket job that's giving me grey hairs.'

Doherty took a packet of cigarettes from his pocket. 'Have a smoke, sir?'

'If you press me this hard, yes.'

They lit their cigarettes. 'Well, Sam?'

Doherty shrugged his shoulders. 'You know as much about things as I do.'

'That's bloody nothing.'

'I wouldn't put it quite like that.'

'I know that. You'd wrap it up in a thick load of Irish bull to try to hide the truth. But I'm telling you, I know nothing, the A.C.C knows nothing, and now it's clear that the investigating D.I knows less than nothing.'

'I'll swear it wasn't a straightforward accident,' said Doherty stubbornly.

'You can swear this and you can swear that, but sweet F.A good that does anyone. Sam, I've nine divisions in this county, each with a D.I with problems. But put all their problems together and it's kid's play compared to your problem. There isn't one of 'em doesn't know whether or not he's got crime in his division. There isn't one of 'em trying to tie a murder charge round the necks of one of the oldest and wealthiest families in the county: so old and so wealthy they can blast you and me right out of our pensions any time they feel like it.'

'It's certainly a bastard.'

'You're not exaggerating.'

'I'll be perfectly frank, sir. We've reached the end of the line. I've tried every avenue and they're all dead-ends. If it was murder, it was one of the good ones.'

Quincy looked down at the electric fire and then tried to move even closer to it. Ash spilled from his cigarette on to the floor. He scuffed it into the worn-out carpet with the toe of his right shoe. 'How d'you make out with the Deckers?'

Doherty thought for a few seconds before answering. 'The old girl's a real character. She's convinced herself that one of her husband's ancestors refused to shoot my ancestors at the time of the uprisings following the potato famines and that's why I'm alive today. She says she's going to search everywhere until she finds the proof. Then it'll show that life moves in circles.'

'Potato famine? What potato famine?'

'D'you mean to say you don't know what went on in Ireland in the last century?'

'Hell, Sam, there isn't time in this world to worry about what you heathen Irish did in the days when you painted yourselves with woad and ate each other.'

'It was the English who used woad and the Welsh who practised cannibalism.'

Quincy looked at his wrist-watch. 'It's nine twenty-five and I'm due in Maidstone at five past ten for some goddamn' conference and I don't think I'll ever make it. All right, Sam, so this case has got to have the shutters put up on it. Put 'em up. But don't let the coroner's court make anything of it, eh? We don't want that bloke making trouble.'

'I'll do the best I can to keep him quiet.'

Quincy stepped away from the fire. 'I wonder how that bloke really died.'

★ ★ ★ ★

The guns gathered at Hurstley Place.

The vast American cars were parked to the right of the porch and the lone Morris 1000 was parked on the left.

At 9.25, Fawcett guided his wheel-chair down the stone steps on to the drive. He muttered a 'good morning' in reply to Abbott's fulsome greeting. Julian drove one Land-Rover round from the yard and Henry Decker drove the other. They climbed down on to the drive. Barbara came out of the house and crossed to speak to Julian. Wade also approached Julian, in company with another man.

'Good morning, Miss Harmsworth, 'morning Decker,' said Wade. 'May I introduce Christopher Lenton, who's coming out with us today.'

Julian shook hands with a florid, portly man who was taking over Rafferty's gun. After a few conversational words of greeting, Julian took a small, round silver case from his pocket and lifted off the lid. Inside were seven numbered silver spills. Each gun drew a spill which gave him the the number of his first stand.

'Where are we going today?' asked Abbotts, as he replaced the spill he had drawn.

'We start at Deer Leap. They've brought

in two shaws and all the fields of kale so there should be a good showing of birds. Who's number one?'

'I am,' said Lenton.

'You'll be out in the field. Most of your birds will be swinging right and watch out for a fox, there's usually one in this beat. It'll try to break along the hedge.'

'Do I take it we shoot foxes, Mr Decker?'

'There's a stiff fine for anyone who misses one! The hunt have to make do with what we leave and be damned thankful we leave any.' Julian raised his voice. 'O.K, let's get moving. We've got four beats this morning and three this afternoon to get in.'

Abbotts, Cranleigh, Wade, and Lenton went to the first Land-Rover. Julian crossed to the second Land-Rover and slid out of the back a patent ramp which enabled Fawcett in his wheel-chair to be pushed up into the back in the well between the seats. Fawcett secured his gun in the rack, behind the front seats, then did the same with Henry Decker's and Julian's guns. He put the cartridge bags on one of the rear seats. At a word of command from Barbara, Toby jumped up into the back and immediately nuzzled Fawcett's hands. Fawcett, an unusually relaxed expression on his face, stroked the dog's head. Henry Decker, Barbara, and Julian climbed into the front seats.

'Let's hope nothing mucks up today's shoot,' said Julian, as he pressed the self-starter and then checked that four-wheel drive was disengaged.

★ ★ ★ ★

Adams consulted his pocket-watch for the fifth time in as many minutes. Were the guns ever going to be ready? Did they imagine birds could be held for hours without most of them scuttling out of the woods as fast as their legs would carry them? The beaters had begun work at 8.30, bringing the fields into the two shaws and the two shaws into Deer Leap. Jim had stood clear of the shaws to see how many birds were put across into the main woods and he claimed the number was as high as four hundred: but he tended always to see two birds where there was only one. The birds were now in Deer Leap Wood and eight stops were gently tapping trees, fences, or hedges, to keep them from using the known escape routes. But, Adams thought, were those stops doing their jobs? He listened, even though he knew he could not expect to hear them. When he heard nothing, he became convinced all eight were falling down on their jobs. Twenty-five bob and a bottle of beer still didn't keep them tapping and they'd only to pause long enough to light a cigarette and twenty birds could have escaped. In his mind, birds began to pour out of the woods.

He looked as far along the line of waiting beaters as he could see. There were less boys than last time, which was a good thing, but old Moore had recovered from the 'flu and was out, which was a bad thing. Old Moore could pick up a dead pheasant and hide it in one of the inside pockets of the dirty old coat he wore and there wouldn't be the hint of a bulge. Old Moore knew the woods better than anyone bar the keepers and he could easily cache a dozen dead birds to be picked up that night. But refuse to have him out beating and he'd really set out to poach by way of retaliation and then God knows how many he'd wipe up.

The Labrador went too far forward.

Adams shouted, and it slunk back. He looked at his watch again. It was ten to ten. By now, the guns had had enough time to get to their stands twice over. In the old days, before Land-Rovers, guns reached their stands dead on time: Land-Rovers were both a boon and a curse, a curse because guns always thought that with them as transport there was plenty of time to spare before they need get moving.

He heard a single shot.

So the guns were at last ready! He wondered who'd be at numbers 2, 3 and 4, which was where the birds would go today. This shoot was designed to give high birds: the flushing fences were set well back and whenever possible the guns were stood in the shallow valleys. That was fine when the team of guns could handle high birds, but was so much wasted effort when there were men like Abbotts, who'd spent a fortune at shooting schools but never learnt to follow through with his swing.

'O.K,' Adams shouted. 'Keep the line straight up to the ride and then swing.'

He began to tap with his stick, to move forward in a zig-zag, and to encourage his dog to push through the bracken and the brambles. This was one of the more difficult beats because in the middle of it they had to swing round on the left and if the right-hand got too far forward, or lagged behind, the birds escaped.

If only he knew which gun Mr Julian was, he could work the beaters to put the birds over that stand so that at least some were shot.

The line moved forward and despite all Adam's fears, they kept fairly straight. When they swung, they did so almost perfectly.

The guns began to fire. The gun in the field was using both barrels every time and there was never a single shot: that meant he was missing every bird, at least with the first shot. The top gun in the woods was firing both barrels pretty regularly, but there was enough break between the first and second shot to show that the target was different birds: he must be either Mr Julian or Mr Fawcett, or perhaps Mr Henry Decker. Mr Henry Decker was a reasonable shot, streets ahead of any of the Mustavabeers, but not in the same class as Mr Julian or Mr Fawcett. You couldn't expect him to be. He wasn't a real Decker.

There was a heavy flush of birds and

Adams called the line to halt. Someone shouted 'Fox.' Adams quickened the rate of tapping of his stick and swore, as if his words would force the fox out forward before the guns. Foxes and pheasants didn't mix and M.F.Hs were a public nuisance. He called the beaters on. Soon, there were two more heavy, but controlled, flushes. For once, even he had to admit that the birds were flying well, rising in order and not as one great cloud, going forward and then curling round to cross the field to the next wood. Two, 3 and 4 guns would have hot barrels. Before the last war it had always been double guns, but those were the days when five thousand birds were put into the woods.

They reached the end of the beat and the hedge that bounded the field. Adams yelled at the beaters to drive the hedge itself and another half-dozen pheasants got up. The new gun was in the field and to Adam's complete disgust he clean missed the two birds that went straight over his head. Two of the remaining four went down the field and curled over the guns, where one was shot, two curled immediately and were missed by number 3 and both brought down by number 2.

Abbotts climbed over the hedge into the field. He picked up a dead hen and the gun in the field called out that there was a cock somewhere about twenty yards to the right. And that, thought Adams disgustedly, seemed to be the sum total of number 1's bag. He spat. He found and picked up the second bird and then went down the field and climbed back into the woods level with number 5 gun. Toby, Miss Harmsworth's dog, flashed past him with a runner in his mouth. The dog wasn't too bad on runners.

He pushed through the bracken and came round one of the fir trees to number 5 stand. He hoped someone would give him news of a dead fox. Then, as he stepped round a chest high patch of brambles, he saw a body on the ground.

CHAPTER 9

Lydia, Henry Decker, Barbara, Fawcett and Julian were in the red withdrawing-room. Lydia and Barbara sat on the large settee to the left of the fireplace and were hardly warmed by the roaring fire. Henry Decker stood between the fireplace and the right-hand wall, Julian stood by the table in front of the french windows. Fawcett had moved his wheel-chair across to the billiards table and was playing with snooker balls, throwing them along the table. One went with such force that it jumped up on hitting the cushion and landed on the floor with a crash that made them all start.

'The fat bastard,' said Fawcett. He aimed the last ball, the black, at the end pocket and threw it. It hit the cushion to the right of the pocket, rebounded, and rolled to a halt just beyond his reach. He dragged himself out of the chair to try to lean over and get the ball and lost his balance. He fell back on to the chair and from there to the floor.

Julian hurried forward, but came to a stop as Fawcett angrily demanded to be left alone. Lydia shivered and looked away so that no one should see the expression on her face.

After a while, Julian spoke. 'It's an impossible coincidence.'

Fawcett, using the immense strength in his arms and shoulders, pulled himself up the side of the chair and swung himself into it.

'He...he might have had an accident,' suggested Barbara.

'Sheer wishful thinking,' said Fawcett. 'The blind human reluctance to face up to the facts if they're nasty. Julian's quite right: the coincidence is impossible. Abbotts was murdered. And so, I congratulate the murderer. After Rafferty, he's the man I'd have next nominated for an early death.'

'Please don't speak like that, Fawcett,' said Lydia.

'Why not? I never did believe in the overworked tag, *de mortuis nil nisi bonum*. Death doesn't recklessly sprinkle sanctity over the corpse. Abbotts was fat and oily. He lived on beer, lavatory stories, and the boozy envy of anyone he could persuade to drink with him. Death hasn't turned him into a saint.'

'Perhaps not,' said Henry Decker, 'but it's probably best not to underline the fact too hard.'

'Not so, Cousin?'

'Not so, Cousin.'

'Surely you're not going to tell me that it's the evil and not the good which gets buried with the man?' Fawcett spoke more quietly. He had always respected Henry Decker for a man with a lot of common-sense—even if that common-sense had forsaken him at the time of his marriage so that he had married a shrew.

'I'm concerned with the living. If Abbotts was murdered, someone murdered him.'

'Your logic is quite unassailable.'

'The police will be investigating. They might mis-understand you and take some of the things you say in the wrong light.'

'Would that matter? Suppose I killed Abbotts: shot him in his fat, stupid, blubbery head. I'm arrested, tried, found guilty, and sentenced to life imprisonment. Where would they imprison me, since I am only complete when with my wheelchair? And how soon will my body make a mockery of their sentence?'

'Stop it,' said Lydia, her voice high.

'Please, please don't talk like that,' pleaded Barbara.

As Fawcett looked at Barbara, the harsh lines about his mouth eased. 'I'm sorry, my child. I was completely forgetting my manners. Will you forgive your contrite future brother-in-law?'

She nodded her head, but uncertainly,

plainly not knowing whether Fawcett was mocking her, or not.

'I know it was just an accident,' said Lydia. 'The most astonishing coincidences happen every day. A friend of mine was out riding and the horse put its foot down a rabbit hole and pitched her off. She broke two of her left ribs. Now who'd believe that?'

'Where's the coincidence?' asked Fawcett.

'That it could happen to two friends of mine in one week.'

'You've only mentioned one set of broken ribs, Mother.'

'Nonsense. The trouble with you, Fawcett, is that you won't listen. Just like your father. I used to tell him something and I'd know very well he wasn't listening so I'd question him about what I'd just said and quite often he couldn't answer even a single question. Barbara, dear, that reminds me. I've heard of a wonderful firm for your wedding reception. They do absolutely everything and even send polite congratulatory telegrams if you think you may not get enough. They're a little bit expensive, but I'm sure your father won't be worried by that. I wrote their name down on a piece of paper and put the paper somewhere safe, but just for the moment I've forgotten where. As soon as I find it, I'll give it to you.'

'The detective has asked us all to hang around so that he can have a word with us,' said Julian.

'Julian,' snapped Lydia, 'you're more annoying than ever. You know very well I was trying to change the conversation.'

'It's a little difficult to forget what's just happened.'

'It doesn't matter how difficult, you've got to try. It's like the story of the Egyptian who was promised wealth to make him the richest man in the world provided he did not think of fish for an hour. Of course, being an Egyptian he immediately thought of fish. They're a feckless race. When your father and I visited the country, we had a terrible job trying to find some honest and industrious boys.'

'Did you hear him have any shots, Henry?' asked Julian.

Lydia stood up. 'I'm going to go and make some coffee and by the time I come back I hope you'll all have found the manners not to discuss the matter for another second.' She quickly walked out of the room.

Fawcett propelled his chair across from the billiards table to the settee. 'How long are we supposed to wait on the detective's pleasure?'

No one answered him. He put the same question to Henry Decker that Julian had done earlier. 'Did you hear Abbotts fire a single shot?'

'Damned if I can really say. You know what it's like once the birds are coming: you're concentrating so hard on them that you're not really conscious of anything or anybody else.'

'What about before the birds really started coming?'

'There were several odd shots, weren't there? Those high pigeons came over and all departed unscathed. They must have had a few shots fired at them and I'd have said Abbotts had his fair share, but it could have been Wade.'

'Is Abbotts married?' asked Barbara.

'No,' replied Julian. 'He was the eternal jolly bachelor, with an inexhaustible fund of tales about nights out with the girls.'

'But why should anyone want to shoot him?'

'God knows.' Rafferty and Abbotts, thought Julian. The first death might or might not have been part of a pattern, but the second death blueprinted that pattern. How much were the police going to find out this time? Now they knew it must be murder, their investigations would be far more intensive, so could they fail to discover the truth? Was it to be good-bye to Hurstley Place, to this huge room with moulded plaster ceiling, to the portraits of long dead Deckers with their long, lean faces? He looked across the room at his brother. Why in the name of hell hadn't Fawcett realised this? he thought wildly.

★ ★ ★ ★

Doherty walked slowly down the field, ten feet from the trees. Behind those trees, grown to make the birds lift high, were the stands, amongst the same kind of undergrowth as King's Beat. Adams had said what a strange coincidence it was that the deaths had taken place at the only two beats where the guns stood amongst so much covert. Coincidence nothing. The killer had used these two beats because they were the only two where he could move unseen from stand to stand.

The new gun, Lenton, had been in the

field and one of the stops had been able to check that Lenton had never moved away from his stand. He was the only one who could be eliminated as a suspect.

Doherty came to a halt by the wooden gate and lit a cigarette. Here he was, thinking about eliminating suspects before the death could be named murder. Abbotts was sprawled on the ground, very much as Rafferty had been. The ground around his head was soaked in blood. His gun, a best London sidelock ejector with superb engraving, had pitched forward in a similar manner to Rafferty's. So just suppose the pathologist said this could have been an accident and the gun expert said this could have been an accident—what then? Two deaths like these could not be accidents—the odds against such a coincidence were far too high—but how did you prove they were murders if you had no more evidence to use than with Rafferty's death?

Doherty shook his head. He was stupid to meet trouble half-way and in any case although one murder might be perfect, two almost certainly couldn't be. Then he thought of all the well-known cases of multiple murder where it was only the fifth, sixth, even tenth murder before the murderer made his first detectable mistake.

He climbed over the gate at the hinge end, careful not to put any weight on the broken top bar, and walked a short way along the main ride to the smaller ride which wound through the undergrowth and around trees from which the guns went to their stands.

At number 5 stand, photographs had been taken, sketches had been made, the doctor had gone, the gun had been taken to Ashford, the body had been carried away in a Land-Rover to the plain undertaker's van, and now only some white tape, pegged in the shape of the body, marked what had happened.

One of the searching constables saw him and came over to him. 'Sir.'

'What?'

'I've found what could be a track, only it's faint.'

Doherty was shown the track which was at the end of the path that went from the ride to the stand. The constable had been only too correct when he said it was faint; it was very faint.

Doherty called for something to kneel

on. When his eyes were close to the earth, he could make out the rough shape of the short, shallow depression and he thought that it could have been made by the solid tyre of a wheel-chair. There was little value in this track because it was so indistinct, yet an effort must be made to photograph and then possibly lift an impression of it. There was one chance in a hundred of lifting an impression and one in ten thousand that some distinguishing feature would be discovered.

He stood up and dusted his knees free of the dust that had been on the sacking. He sent the constable off to find Detective Sergeant Orr and tell him to come along and do what he could with the track, then he left and returned to the ride. Fawcett Decker had been at number 7 stand, the one nearest the ride at the bottom of the wood and close to the broken wooden gate. Wade had been at number 6. Doherty walked down the ride and up the path to number 6 stand. In the small clearing was a stick with its red marker in the top and on the ground were a large number of empty cartridges. He picked up a handful. All were Westley-Richards and all were number $6\frac{1}{2}$ shot. He turned round. From here, the ride was not visible and a person coming along could easily conceal himself by stooping—or by being in a wheel-chair. Even if someone had walked along upright, Wade would probably have missed him. Wade would have been concentrating on the birds.

Doherty returned to the ride and went down it, past number 7 stand, to the gate. Detective Sergeant Orr reached the gate, from the opposite direction, at the same moment. He lifted his photographic equipment over the gate. 'I was just on my way home,' he said, 'this being a Saturday.'

'And now you're not. That's what makes for a tough life.'

'It's that all right.'

'Just don't weaken.'

Orr climbed over the gate.

'See what you can do with the imprint in the ground,' said Doherty. 'It'll need a miracle to make anything of it, so arrange a miracle.'

'Yes, sir. I'm hot on miracles on a Saturday afternoon.'

'It's a tough life,' replied Doherty, for the second time. After Orr had gone up the ride, he leaned against the gate and lit a cigarette. With cigarettes at their present astronomical price, he couldn't afford to smoke, but a case like the present one would make a chain smoker out of anyone.

What would the pathologist and gun expert have to say? Would they be able to prove this a murder?

★ ★ ★ ★

Doherty drove up to Hurstley Place and climbed out of his car. The late afternoon sky was solid with cloud which from time to time shed showers of sleet. He looked up at the house and saw it now not as an ugly pile of bricks and mortar, but as a house strong enough to endure through the ages.

He knocked on the door and stood below the almost frightening heraldic beast carved in the stone. A woman opened the door and he correctly identified her as the wife of the butler-cum-handyman. She was plump, almost fat, had a very dark complexion, and her jet black hair was tied back severely into a bun. He asked if he could speak to Mr Fawcett Decker. She left him in the hall and went off in the direction of the drawing-rooms.

He corrected his thoughts. Withdrawing-rooms. He was faintly surprised to discover that it now seemed right and natural that here the ancient name for the rooms should have been maintained in face of all common usage. The Deckers did not need to bother about common usage.

Lydia Decker came into the hall. She was wearing a tweed suit that was clearly all but worn out. In direct contrast, she had round her neck a double row of pearls, beautifully matched and graded, which Doherty did not doubt were natural pearls and worth a fortune.

'Good afternoon, Mr Doherty. There, I've remembered your name, haven't I?'

'Yes, Mrs Decker, you have.'

'I know my memory isn't as bad as some people will try to make out. Only two weeks ago...'

'I'm sorry to bother you, but is Mr Fawcett Decker in?'

She ignored the question. 'You've just reminded me. I've been searching the records, Mr Doherty, and Peverill Decker refused to shoot his pistol or order a charge near Castlereagh. Is that where your grandfather would have joined the uprising?'

'They used to live in County Galway.'

'The very next county. Obviously, the famine had sent them wandering in a desperate search for food. I feel convinced now that your ancestors and mine faced each other: if you will allow that they are my ancestors—as I told you, the Awcotts are distinctly related to the Deckers. Who was the poet who said that each meeting is simply the tangible proof of the great tapestry of life into which we are all woven?'

'I'm afraid I don't...'

'Or was it one of those tiresome gentlemen who used to write aphorisms and epigrams in order to appear in the reference books of quotations? I'm convinced that that odious Mr Johnson wouldn't even say good morning until he was satisfied Boswell was ready to start writing. Epigrams always get so dusty. There was an Amelia Decker who kept a diary in the middle of the eighteenth century and it would have been a very interesting record had she not insisted on larding every other sentence with a sanctimonious epigram.'

'Can I...'

'I'm certain a diary should be short and

sharp and preferably scandalous. Pepys's diary really is the perfect example. The man must have been a little monster, but...'

'Mrs Decker, I'm afraid it's no good.'

'No good?' she repeated, in surprise.

'I have to speak to Mr Fawcett Decker.'

'Oh!' She fingered her pearls. 'You're a very insistent man.'

'I'm afraid that it's my job to be.'

'It's the Irish blood in you. The Irish have deliberately projected the popular conception of their character as totally irresponsible as a kind of smoke-screen. In reality, they're nothing of the sort...'

'Is he in?'

Lydia Decker sighed. Doherty was suddenly struck by the fact that she was looking old and slightly crumpled, as if life had come up from behind and struck her a crippling blow. 'He's very ill,' she said.

'I'm sorry to hear this. It's rather sudden?'

'His illness is like that.'

'But it's only this morning that he was out shooting.'

She sighed again, looked at him for several seconds, then crossed the hall.

When she saw he had not moved, she asked him to follow her. By the door, she picked up a silver salver from an oak chest and moved it slightly to the right. 'The Danellis simply will not put things back after dusting,' she said. She led the way into the green withdrawing-room and asked him to wait.

Alone, Doherty slowly looked round the room. It was filled with *objets d'art*. On the walls hung framed needlework and paintings and two rows of miniatures, two glass-fronted cupboards were filled with glass or crystal goblets, there were silver ornaments on the many small tables, silver candelabra on the upright piano, and the shelves of a Welsh-dresser were crowded with china figures which looked to him very old and were probably very valuable.

There was sound from the doorway and he turned to see Fawcett Decker manoeuvre his wheel-chair into the room.

'You wanted to see me?' demanded Fawcett, in a challenging manner.

'Yes, sir.'

'In connection with what?'

'The death of Mr Abbotts.'

'Another regrettable accident.'

'Regretted by whom?'

'A good question, Inspector. His death is not regretted by me, for one. I considered him an evil bore.'

'Evil?'

'He was too thick-skinned to realise he bored people. There's nothing more evil than that.'

Doherty studied the lean, dark face of Fawcett Decker, with its expression of bitter cynicism and pain. The poor bastard, thought Doherty, to be stuck forever in that chair. Wealth might have cushioned his distress, but on the other hand it might just as easily not have done so: the anguish would be in his mind and his mind would dictate how much anguish he felt, not his surroundings. 'I wonder if you can help, sir, over what happened?'

'How can I? Unless, of course, you think I killed him?'

'There's no question yet, sir, of it being murder.'

'You make a poor liar,' Fawcett spoke jeeringly.

'That's what my wife always claims.'

'If I did murder him, Inspector, and it can be proved, I'll set a lot of people a lot of problems, won't I? How can I be fitted into the routine of prison? Will I ever be allowed out of the hospital? How can a total cripple be disciplined? I'm a walking miracle because the doctors killed me off I don't know how many years ago: but a miracle is easily shattered.'

'I'm sorry, sir.'

'I appreciate the irony in your sympathy at a time when you're trying to discover whether I murdered the fat, sweating, boorish Mr Abbotts.'

'Did you go straight to your stand from the car, sir?'

'The ramp was attached to the tail of the Land-Rover and then, with my usual skill, I disembarked and propelled myself to number seven stand.'

'That's the bottom one?'

'You are quite correct.'

'Did you leave that stand at all?'

'If I murdered Abbotts, I surely must have done?'

'You're making it rather difficult for me, sir.'

'In the circumstances, you can hardly expect me to make things easy for you.'

'Did you leave your stand at all during the beat, sir?'

'You must have a good reason for asking?'

'Perhaps.'

'What is it?'

'That doesn't matter for the moment.'

'On the contrary, it matters a very great deal.'

'Mr Decker, what was Rafferty threatening your family with?' Doherty watched Fawcett's expression become hard, almost cruel. 'Would you mind telling me,' he persisted, when there was no answer.

'You're mistaken.'

'I don't think so.'

'That's your privilege.'

'Was the threat to the whole family, to you, or to your brother?'

'Do you think I killed Rafferty and Abbotts?'

'I'm trying to find out what happened, nothing more.'

'What makes you think I left my stand during the beat?'

'There's a mark at number five stand that could have been made by the tyre of a wheel-chair.'

'But was it?'

'I...I am not yet certain, sir.'

'Then you want me to admit to a visit

you cannot yet prove? If I murdered Abbotts I certainly wouldn't make such an admission and if I did not murder him I equally would make no such admission as how could I then hope to prove my innocence?'

'It always pays to tell the truth, sir.'

'That is stupid. It seldom pays to tell the truth.'

'Then you're not going to answer me?'

'Ask me again when you're quite certain what did make that track.'

Doherty spoke slowly. 'I didn't expect this visit to achieve anything.'

'Then you're in the unusual, but happy, position of being able to go away utterly undisappointed. You did say you were about to leave, didn't you, Inspector?'

Doherty walked slowly towards the door, hesitated by it, and then went out and left the house.

In the smaller kitchen, now used to house the deep freeze, refrigerator, and washing machine, Lydia Decker tried for the fifth time to arrange five roses in a long-stemmed glass vase. Lucretia Danelli offered to help, but was summarily dismissed from the room. Almost immediately afterwards, Julian entered.

'Is he still here?' asked Lydia. She tried to move one rose slightly to the left and in her nervousness disturbed all of them.

'They were in the green room a minute or so ago.'

'Julian, you must go in and see what's happening. You know what Fawcett can be like. He's probably being very rude to the detective and that's not a good thing. Your dear father said that it never paid to be rude to even the most junior policeman because he'd always get his own back. I remember when we went...'

'It's better if I stay out of there.'

'Don't you want to help your brother?'

'How can I?'

'I've just explained and if you'd only listen to me...'

'Then you think Fawcett shot Abbotts?'

Lydia very carefully began to arrange the roses once more.

'Do you think he shot him, Mother?'

'Fawcett would never do such a thing.'

'Not to save this place?'

'Fawcett didn't shoot that man and I refuse to discuss such a horrible thought. You're not to talk like that, Julian, or you'll upset me very badly.'

'Wouldn't it be better to get it out in

the open and talk about it?'

'Certainly not. I can't think how Barbara will live with you if you're as tiresome with her as you are with me.'

'But you can't ignore the thing into non-existence: and you can't drown it in a flood of words. You want me to go in to the green room and stop Fawcett's being so indiscreet as to admit to the two murders you're sure he committed. That's the truth, isn't it?'

'Julian, you're being especially horrid and if you can think that sort of thing about your brother, you're also especially disloyal.'

Julian stared at his mother. She was frightening herself sick with her fears and yet even now she would not admit to them because she wanted to make him believe such fears were ridiculous.

He left and went through the large kitchen to the butler's pantry and then into the dining-room. Danelli was laying the table. Julian crossed to one of the six tall french windows. He looked out at the countryside and saw the sheep, the herd of Jerseys, the kale the pigeons were beginning to attack, the small copse where there was a large badger set and had been for as long as anyone could remember, and in the distance the hills. From here, neither Avonley nor Ashford was visible and there was no sign of the ever-spreading rash of building which was engulfing Kent. The scene was one of peace. Yet, beyond the copse was Deer Leap Wood and there a man had been shot dead.

Surely this second death must shatter the Decker heritage, even though the first, by some miracle, had failed to do so?

CHAPTER 10

Doherty drove to Ashford on Monday morning and parked in the main council car-park. He went up the narrow passage by the Odeon Cinema to the High Street and into Hutsons to buy a tin of anchovies for Peggy, who considered them the greatest treat life had to offer. He then walked to the traffic lights and along the crowded pavements to the mortuary.

The pathologist had begun work. Doherty stared at the flabby body of Abbotts and wondered whether the man had known any terror before he was shot, or whether everything had happened far too quickly for that.

Some time later, the pathologist gave a hurried report. 'There's nothing definite, Inspector. I can say that it's certainly not suicide, but although it was probably murder it could have been an accident. Almost exactly the same considerations apply here as with the last killing and all the figures are near enough the same. I'll make out a full report and let you have it when I can, but my secretary's ill and I'm far too rushed to waste time typing.'

'This could have been an accident?'

'As I have just said, yes. Purely on the evidence of the body there is nothing finally to prove it was not an accident.'

Doherty spoke reflectively. 'Whatever the medical evidence, a jury's unlikely to believe in two accidents like these.'

'My experience of juries leads me to be prepared for them to believe anything, provided only that it's illogical to do so. However, their beliefs are not my worry. Good-bye, Inspector. I have another two P.M.s to carry out and someone else will have to shunt this corpse on. The human race at the moment wisely seems bent on exterminating itself.' The pathologist hurried out of the room.

Doherty went through to one of the small rooms, in which Williams was working. Williams, weighing shot in a pair of laboratory scales, looked round.

'Close the door, man. A draught like that upsets everything.'

Doherty shut the door. He watched Williams add another tiny weight to one pan and then raise both pans by pressing down the central control lever. They rose and quivered slightly before settling into equilibrium. Williams lowered the pans. He wrote in his note-book, after which he carefully emptied the shot into a plastic bag which he packed into a cardboard box. He sealed the box and scribbled a signature on it.

'Any luck?' asked Doherty.

'Luck? Luck has no part in my work.'

Hell, thought Doherty, the man's really pompous today. 'What I mean sir, is that...'

'Inspector, the science of firearms and ballistics is perhaps the most exact in the whole field of forensic investigation.'

'I'm sure it is, sir.'

Williams moved away from the worktable and stood in the centre of the room. He thrust his chin forward and, luckily unknown to him, irresistibly reminded the D.I of a bantam cockerel on a dung heap. 'Inspector, certain facts are inescapable. With this killing the whole of the charge entered the body and on my explicit directions every pellet has been recovered.'

The pathologist would like to know he had been 'directed,' thought Doherty.

'The size of the shot is again number five and there are two hundred and one pellets, weighing just under fifteen-sixteenths of an ounce. On the presumption that a very few pellets have inevitably been irretrievably lost, we have the standard load for a two and a half inch sixteen bore cartridge.'

'Sixteen bore?'

'That is so, Inspector.'

'How does this fit in with the cartridges I brought you?'

Williams turned round, opened a small leather case, and brought out from it seven cartridges which he set up on their bases. Around each cartridge was a tag. 'Here they are, Inspector. All are two and a half-inch, all are standard loads, and none is a maximum cartridge. All are five shot except for one which is six and a half: incidentally, I do not agree that a half size gives the advantages claimed. The twelve bore cartridges have a shot load of one and one sixteenth and one and one eighth ounces.

'One and one sixteenth ounces hold two hundred and thirty-four pellets, one and one eighth ounces holds two hundred and forty-eight... I'm talking about number five shot, of course. The pathologist is quite certain that it is impossible he has missed as many as thirty-three pellets. Therefore, I can tell you that the deceased was killed by the load from a sixteen bore cartridge.'

'Since his gun was a twelve bore, we can rule out accident?'

'That is an inescapable conclusion.'

'And only two sixteen bore guns were being used.'

'Quite so.'

'Would you expect the average shot, sir, to realise that the size of the gun he was using could be judged from the number of pellets found in a body?'

'I would very much doubt it. And remember, this can only happen when nothing but standard load cartridges are being used. Have you collected every cartridge case found at the dead man's stand?'

'There were only a lot of pretty old ones.'

'Let me see them, please.' Williams, for a few seconds, tapped his teeth with his forefinger. 'In fact, I had better examine every cartridge from every stand so that we can answer any defence allegations of non-standard load cartridges giving a different load of shot.'

'I'll get on to that right away, sir.'

Both men stared at the cartridges on the table, two of which were thinner than the remaining five. Only the two brothers had shot with sixteen bore guns.

★ ★ ★ ★

Detective Constable Pawley knocked on the brightly coloured door of Abbotts's house in Yarnley-without. As he waited, he watched a large black bird circle the square steeple of the church and he wondered, in a vague way, what kind of bird it was. The door was opened by a blonde. Pawley, who hadn't seen her on his first visit to the house, gazed with open appreciation. The D.I had said there was a housekeeper and that she'd obviously kept more than just the house warm, but he hadn't gone on to say what a perfect dish she was. Probably the D.I was too old to appreciate such things any more.

'Yes?' said the blonde, distantly. She had no doubt about where the caller's thoughts were wandering.

'Detective Constable Pawley at your service.'

'What d'you want?'

'A few soft words.'

'I suppose you'd better come on in, then. But you'll have to hurry, mind. I'm off soon.'

'Off to where?'

'Off out. There ain't much use to staying here, is there?'

Pawley stepped into the hall. She shut the door and waited, a disinterested expression on her face.

'We're trying to find out all we can about Abbotts,' said Pawley.

'Why go to the trouble? D'you want to know something? He's left me without a brass farthing. After all I did for him.'

'Did you?'

'You've a filthy mind.'

'I know—but it's fun.'

'For who?'

'Now you're asking. How long have you been here?'

'Three months and I was a fool, I don't mind admitting, He liked to chuck his money around in front of other people, but back here with no one to look on what he was doing, he'd worry about spending sixpence. There was a little bracelet in Canterbury I saw and I asked him to get it for me, but would he? Like heck. You can't get meaner than that.'

'I'd buy it for you.'

'What makes you think I'd give you the chance?'

'Try me out for size,' he leered.

She studied him with a cool regard. 'On a copper's pay?' she finally asked with scorn.

You bitch, thought Pawley appreciatively. 'Did he ever talk about the Deckers?'

'He used to curse them, if that's what you mean.'

'He never mentioned any kind of secret about them?'

'What the hell are you talking about?'

'Or he never chatted about what Rafferty knew concerning 'em?'

'Look, chum, Joe and me had better

things to talk about than the Deckers or Rafferty.'

If she had only been in the house for three months, she obviously knew nothing about what had happened before the end of July. 'Any idea whether Abbotts had a housekeeper before you came here?'

'Strike a light, you ask some bloody silly questions for a detective. A bloke like him doesn't live alone until he's dead.'

'Who was here before?'

'Someone with the sense to clear out when the going was good. D'you know, a solicitor comes here and gives me a month's wages and tells me to hop it as if if he was ordering a bit of dirt around. I told him just what I thought...'

'D'you have any idea who was here before?'

'And what if I do?'

'Then you can give me her name and address.'

'You're out of luck, mate.'

'But you just implied you knew.'

'I didn't imply nothing. What happened is, I found some photos. They was the kind you wouldn't show to your aunt, and that's a fact. The girl in 'em was the last housekeeper.'

'What happened to the photos?'
'They're still around, I suppose.'
'Perhaps you could find 'em?'
'Perhaps.'
'You've no idea where the girl lives?'
'I just know she moved on to Maidstone.'
'How d'you know that?'
'You look after your business and I'll look after mine.'
'All right, all right. Now suppose you go and find those photos.'
'I don't know you're old enough to see 'em,' she said, as insultingly as possible, before she left.

★ ★ ★ ★

In Maidstone, detectives began the laborious task of trying to identify and find the girl in the photographs. Through a mixture of hard work and good luck, they succeeded after only two days. Doherty drove up to Maidstone and, in company with one of the divisional detectives, went to the house where she was living.

Thelma was a brunette with a strikingly beautiful face and a figure that could wear any bikini. She spoke with a lisp that at first was rather attractive but which quite soon became irritating. She agreed, without any sign of embarrassment, that she was the girl in the photographs. She said she had left Abbotts because of 'better opportunities.'

'A girl's got to live,' she said, and played with the large diamond ring on her finger.

'Of course,' said Doherty. 'How d'you get on with Joe Abbotts? Did you like him?'

She regarded the D.I and her big brown eyes seemed to widen a little. 'What a funny question.'

'I...why...' said Doherty, unable for the moment to say anything more coherent.

'He wasn't very sympathetic, if you know what I mean. And also he was a little mean.' She looked down at her diamond ring.

Both the D.I and the divisional detective thought that if the diamond was genuine, she now had no cause to complain about opportunities.

'I suppose you met Bill Rafferty?' said Doherty.

'Once or twice.' Reluctantly, she let go of the ring. She brushed some hair away from her forehead. 'I didn't like him. He always seemed a little cruel to me.'

'Did they ever talk about the Decker family?'

'Sometimes it seemed as if when they was together they never talked about anything else. Bill was the one, though. It was daft. When a bloke has as much money as him, what's he got to worry about? From the way he'd go on, you'd think he was a little boy. Like the time he kept on boasting. They'll have to do with us now, he kept saying, and stuff their bloody airs and graces.'

'When was this?'

'During the summer, I guess. It must have been, mustn't it, 'cause I was only with Joe from February. We were in the sitting-room, drinking. Joe used to drink like his stomach hadn't a bottom to it. Don't drink so much, Joe, I'd say. Try holding back Niagara, he'd answer and laugh like a drain.'

'Can you remember anything else they said at that time?'

'Not really. You know what it's like when you're drinking and there's a bloke around you wouldn't call your best pal. You don't listen. I could do Joe, but not Bill Rafferty. When I read he'd shot himself, I thought it was a good thing. It'll give his wife a chance, won't it? She'll be rich and able to enjoy life. It's funny how people get together. Joe and Bill wasn't a bit alike, but they chummed up and not just for work. They even went abroad together, just the two of 'em. I mean, if me and Daphne had gone as well it would've made more sense, wouldn't it?'

'I suppose it would have done. When was this?'

'Wasn't all that long ago. In the summer, I guess. Whilst they was gone, I got lonely and met my friend.' She played with the diamond ring once more.

'Can you remember which month you left Abbotts?'

'About August.'

'They'll have gone abroad just before that, then?'

'That's right.'

'Have you any idea where they went?'

'I did hear, but the name of the place was odd and I've forgotten it.'

'Is there any chance of digging back in your memory and recalling it?' Doherty did not, at that moment, think the answer would hold any special significance.

She pursed her mouth and when she spoke her lisp was more apparent than before. 'It was in France. A kind of a funny name... Something like plimsolls, I guess.'

Doherty wondered how tortured was her pronunciation? He vaguely tried to think of towns in France beginning with P. Paris, Perpignan, and Perigueux were the only ones he could remember. Then, as he was about to move on to another question, there came to him a fourth name: Plincennes. 'Was it Plincennes?'

She stared at him. 'You're right! Now isn't that clever of you.'

★ ★ ★ ★

Quincy's room at H.Q was large and airy and he shared it with one of the two H.Q detective chief inspectors. When Doherty went in, only Quincy was present.

The detective superintendent leaned back in his chair. 'What have you got to tell me that won't give me heart failure or apoplexy?'

'Not much, sir, that wasn't in my last written report.'

'Then you're running true to form, Sam, and there's a fact. I saw the A.C.C yesterday. He demanded a report on the Decker business and I told him that nothing on this earth would give me greater pleasure than to be able to give him one, but that until my D.I took all eight fingers out it didn't look as if anyone would ever know anything.'

'What were his reactions?'

'He blew his cheeks out, got a bit red in the face, and asked me how you and I liked the force and whether we meant to stay on in it.' Quincy jerked himself forward. 'Sam, I've a wife and kids and I want to live to enjoy my pension with them. So make some progress, but make it safe, eh?'

'I want to go to France, sir.'

'What the hell for?'

'I don't really know.'

Quincy stood up and walked round his desk. 'Sam, against my better judgement I like you, but so help me, I could take you by your Irish neck and throttle you. I'm on the rack because I'm stupid enough to have the faith in you to leave you to run the Decker case and all you can do is...'

'Abbotts and Rafferty went this summer, on their own and leaving wives and girl-friends behind, to a place in France called Plincennes.'

'So am I supposed to get all excited?'

'The Decker father died in Plincennes in nineteen-fifty-nine.'

Quincy returned to his chair and sat down. He picked up a ruler and slapped it against the palm of his hand. 'And?'

'And nothing definite, sir. But there must be a connection. Because I can't see the connection yet, I must go over rather than put through the usual request for information.'

'It could just be a coincidence.'

'Like the coincidence of Rafferty and Abbotts both being "accidentally" killed in precisely the same way?'

'If you don't know what you're looking for, how the hell do we frame the request to the French police?'

'I think that's your pigeon, sir, since you're the boss.'

'Trust an Irishman to stab a bloke in the back.'

'If he does stab a friend or two, sir, there's usually a very good cause.'

★ ★ ★ ★

Julian was down by the water meadows. The farms here were all let and because the land was frequently flooded during the winter it was held officially that the rent must be very low: three pounds an acre. Yet the flooding covered the land with rich alluvial deposits that made the grass grow in the summer almost as if it were corn: the tenants sub-let fields at up to twenty pounds an acre and so showed a very considerable unearned profit.

Julian watched several wigeon rise from the river, nowhere near flooding level, and fly downwind. He wondered what had disturbed them, then saw the head of Doherty appear above a fold in the ground.

'Good morning, sir,' said Doherty, when within speaking distance. 'It's a cold wind today, like the forecast said it would be.'

'Yes.'

'I'm sorry to come along to bother you, but there's a question I must ask.'

'What's that?'

'Which members of your family went over to France when your father died?'

Julian shivered. He stared again at the water meadows, but this time he was no longer wondering when the estate could either regain possession of them or else charge an economic rent: he was wondering whether they would even belong to the estate in a few months' time.

'Did you go over there?' asked Doherty.

Julian turned. The blue eyes of the detective would have missed none of his reactions to the questions. Not that it really mattered, he thought, what they had seen. The detective must have begun to uncover the truth or he would never have put the question.

'Did you?' persisted Doherty.

'I went to France, yes.'

'Before he died?'

'Yes.'

'I'm sorry to keep prying, but where was he buried?'

'In Plincennes, where he died.'

'Isn't it usual...I mean, his body wasn't brought back to the family burial ground?'

'There's a tradition in the family of being buried in the country in which one dies,' said Julian harshly.

'Did any other members of the family go to France, sir?'

'My mother and my brother attended the funeral.'

'Thank you very much for telling me, sir.'

'Have you...' began Julian, but stopped

himself. The detective waited for a moment, said good-bye, turned and left. Julian inconsequentially thought how mournful Doherty's mournful face had been looking.

Julian walked along the river bank to the road, half a mile away. He felt sick, as if someone had hit him in the stomach. What would Fawcett's reactions now suggest? Would the inevitable disaster break his mother, or would her tough spirit prove even greater than he had ever believed it to be? Yet surely she could not see the Deckers lose Hurstley Place and retain her faith?

He reached the road and the parked Vauxhall shooting brake. One of the tenants shouted a greeting as he climbed into the car. That farmer, as had his father before him, fought the estate as hard as he could, demanding impossibly expensive repairs and insisting that the slightest increase in rent would ruin him. He owned a three litre Rover and his daughter ran two show jumpers.

Julian drove along the lanes to the entrance gates of Hurstley Place and there, acting on impulse, he braked the car to a halt. It suddenly came to him how little he wanted to go back to the house.

He reversed the car on to the road and drove in the general direction of Ashford until he could take a southerly route round the town to Barbara's house. The housekeeper there told him that Miss Harmsworth had left the house about an hour ago, but that she should soon be back.

He thanked the housekeeper and returned to his car, started the engine, and was halfway round the drive when an M.G sports car came in from the road. He stopped and went across to the M.G. Despite the cold, the hood was down and Barbara's hair was tangled and her face was flushed from the wind. In the passenger seat was Toby, looking pompous.

'What a wonderful surprise,' said Barbara. Then she noticed the lines of worry on his face. 'What's wrong, darling?'

'Barbara, let's go up to the Devil's Dyke?'

'Of course. Push Toby into the back seat.'

He climbed into the front after overcoming the dog's resistance to being relegated to the back. Barbara rested her hand on his. 'Is it something to do with us?'

'Not directly.'

'Then it can't be desperate. That's the only thing which would be desperate for me, Julian. You know that, don't you?'

He nodded.

As they drove towards the hills, Julian watched her face. She had strong features, in profile, and these accurately depicted her character. She was intensely loyal and quite unmovable in her defence of someone she loved. When she had first met Lydia Decker there had been a clash of personalities, but there had soon been peace when both women realised how necessary it was for them to get on with each other. Before long, they had grown to respect, and so like, each other.

They climbed the road to the top of the hills and to the Devil's Dyke, as some called it, where the devil was said to have landed on one foot after his fall from Heaven. In summer, this was a noted beauty spot which attracted onlookers by the score, but in winter it was usually deserted, being windy and somewhat desolate.

They parked opposite the centre of the deep fault and for a short while they were silent as they stared down at the view: a mosaic of fields and houses, with the distant sea looking dirty under the ugly grey clouds.

'What's the trouble?' she asked softly.

'The family will soon be in a bit of a stinking mess.'

'Well?'

'I thought you might like to break off while things are still quiet?'

'How d'you mean, Julian?'

'Break off the engagement. As my fiancée, you're bound to get some of the mud flow round you.'

'Is the trouble to do with the two shootings accidents?'

'Partly.'

'They weren't accidents, were they?'

'I doubt it.'

'And you think Fawcett shot them?'

He did not answer.

'Look at me, darling.'

He turned and looked straight at her.

'Don't keep things from me. I don't care what anyone in your family's done, any more than I care what you've done. I'll stand by you whatever's happened. How could you imagine I'd do anything else?'

'You're...you're rather wonderful.'

'I just happen to love you.'

'We could lose Hurstley Place.'

'I'd hate it for your sake, but not quite so much for mine. If we do live there, I'll always feel that one of us is only your mistress.'

He managed a smile. 'They do say that a mistress has a darned good life.'

CHAPTER 11

Doherty had a great fund of common-sense and therefore knew perfectly well that Paris could not match up to the image of Paris in his mind: nevertheless, when he looked around a little of the city and found it so unexciting, he felt disappointed and even a little depressed.

In the afternoon of his arrival, he went to the H.Q of the Sûreté Nationale in the Rue des Saussaies. After a short wait, he was shown into an office on the second floor and introduced to a liaison member of the French National Central Bureau of Interpol. He was received with a formal politeness, but ill-hidden surprise when he admitted that he was not certain what evidence he was looking for. In that case, said his host, would it not be a little difficult to find it? A little difficult, agreed Doherty, but the quality of French help was so high that there could be only one possible outcome to his visit—a satisfactory one. The Frenchman accepted the compliment gracefully, but also with a manner that suggested nothing more than the truth had been spoken. He said that the next day Doherty should go to Plincennes, see the Commissaire de Police, and request such aid as he wanted. If necessary the assistance of the regional Police Judiciaire could also be called for. It was to be hoped that, said the Frenchman, Monsieur Doherty thus would find whatever it was he sought: always provided, of course, he could recognise it when he found it. The Frenchman shook hands with great cordiality.

Later, Doherty went to a nightclub. As he watched an inferior cabaret, he remembered how Peggy had pointedly twice talked about the temptations of Paris. As he paid the grossly inflated bill for the bottle of poor champagne he had had to buy, he sadly wished that at least some of the mythical temptations had been put before him so that he could have had the pleasure of virtuously refusing them.

The next morning, he caught an electric train from the Gare du Nord to Plincennes. A taxi took him to the central police station and there he met the Commissaire de Police, a middle-aged man whose English was as rusty as his French. They shook hands several times and assured each other of a number of things, without understanding what the other said. After a few minutes, a third man, in uniform, came into the room.

The newcomer spoke to the Commissaire, after which he introduced himself to Doherty. He spoke English with a heavy accent. 'Senior Inspector Chauvin. It is a charming occasion to meet you.'

'How d'you do,' replied Doherty, prosaically.

They all sat down. Coffee was brought in.

'Now,' said Chauvin, 'we wish to hear what it is you would like. The boss had a long telephone call from the Directeur de la Police Judiciaire asking us to give you every assistance. We of the Sûreté Urbaine will be delighted to help you in every way. If by some strange chance there is something we cannot accomplish, we shall call in someone from the Police Judiciaire, but in Plincennes we do not usually need to ask for help.' He switched to French and spoke rapidly.

He finished speaking to the commissionaire and looked expectantly at Doherty. Doherty cleared his throat. 'It's a little difficult,' he said.

'Good.'

'The trouble is, I'm not quite certain what I'm looking for.'

'You are not what?'

As briefly as possible, Doherty explained what had happened and how it seemed that two separate trails in the Decker case crossed in Plincennes. 'The two dead men were here this summer,' he finally said, 'and we've been quite unable to find out why they came here. Some years ago, Fawcett Decker, the father, died and was buried here. There must be a connection between these two facts.'

The two Frenchmen spoke together for some few minutes.

'We will investigate the papers of Monsieur Decker's death,' said Chauvin. 'We will also discover where these two men stayed during the past summer.'

'You're very kind.'

'It is a pleasure to assist a friend and workmate from England,' replied Chauvin, not to be outdone in politeness.

Doherty left the police station and walked slowly along the main street. There was a market in the square, before the church, and he wandered amongst the stalls. He bought a hundred grammes of Gruyère and ate it there and then, continued along the street to a café where the pavement tables were protected from the weather by glass screens. Here, he ordered a coffee. As he waited, he wondered whether he would discover anything of importance and, if he did not, how worried he would feel on that score.

* * * *

Chauvin picked up Doherty at the hotel at 4.30 that afternoon. He drove a Peugeot with the brutal skill traditionally ascribed to all Frenchmen.

'We are going to see the doctor who certified death,' he said, as he cut in front of a light van. 'He lives on the Isle.'

'What was the cause of death?'

'Cerebral thrombosis—I looked up in a

dictionary to be able to tell you what the words on the certificate mean.'

'Is the doctor a well-known man?' asked Doherty.

They turned right and descended a sloping yard on either side of which were houses, all in need of some repair.

'Strange, no one seems to have met him recently and we of the police usually meet the doctors often. Perhaps he is old and...out of work, do you say?'

'Retired.'

'Of course.' Chauvin turned right again, almost under the wheels of a heavy lorry, and they came to an area where a number of houses had recently been demolished. Beyond this were canal locks. Chauvin parked the car against some railings and they crossed the bridge over the side-by-side locks, in one of which were two large barges and a small yacht rapidly being raised to the level of the river on the far side. Just before they descended the concrete stairs, Chauvin waved at the man in the control tower, set above the locks, and the latter replied by calling out through the loud hailer.

Once on the island, they walked along the rough road, on either side of which were bungalows, both expensive and cheap in juxtaposition, and a few houses.

'Since some years ago,' said Chauvin, 'this was a place for the not very wealthy to retire. Then it becomes chic to live on a river and a place here costs more than anywhere else in Plincennes. It is strange, because the water...is not clean, do you say?' He stopped and spoke to a woman who was wheeling a suitcase along on a small trolley. She pointed to a white gate a hundred yards farther along. 'We are here,' said Chauvin, as they resumed walking.

The address was a simple wooden bungalow, built up on stilts. It was surrounded by so many trees, mainly evergreens, that as they waited on the balcony they could only just see the river.

A woman opened the front door and spoke to Chauvin. She was middle-aged, with a heavily lined, slightly ugly face, and she wore a badly-stained dress. After a while, she asked them into the house. They went into the sitting-room which was very poorly furnished and cold, despite the paraffin stove that was burning.

Doherty listened to their talking and tried broadly to follow what they were saying, but only occasionally was he able to distinguish a word he could recognise. He walked over to a bookcase and stared at the soft-cover books in it.

'When did this man die?' asked Chauvin suddenly, in English.

Doherty checked the date which was written in his notebook. 'June, nineteen-fifty-nine.'

Chauvin resumed talking to the woman. Doherty wondered where the doctor was now? Did the French have a full national health service or was medicine still efficiently practised and the patient treated with some consideration?

Chauvin interrupted Doherty's scattered thoughts. 'Doctor Roget is dead. It appears his death was entirely natural and due only to his years. We shall check that, of course. He has not been living here for some time because he was a man who loved the sun and so he went to the south to live. This woman here was a cousin and he asked her to live as a kind of...not a servant...'

'Housekeeper?'

'Exactly. She has been his housekeeper. When he died, he gave her this house in his will.'

'Have you been able to find out when he went to the south?'

'He left here in fifty-nine. This woman thinks it was July or August, but of that she is far from certain. She says she can make certain. She says he came into money and that was why he was able to go to the south and live in the sun.'

'Much money?'

Chauvin shrugged his shoulders. 'Of course, she cannot really know. She says a great amount, but then she is a...'

'A bit of a slattern?'

'I would think so. I asked her if the doctor was having plenty of money before he left and she says not. He was too old to make money. New people want doctors who use all the new drugs they read of in the magazines.'

Doherty stared unseeingly out of the window. He heard the single sharp toot of a barge's horn, followed by several toots from another. Was there a pattern? A doctor, too old to make much money, living in a somewhat ramshackle bungalow who suddenly came into enough money to move to the south and yet keep this bungalow: the money coming to him a month or two after Decker's death?

'We shall investigate,' said Chauvin. He brusquely thanked the woman, shook hands with her, and walked to the door. The woman smiled uncertainly at Doherty. He shook hands with her, thought he'd say good-bye in French and then funked even that simple exercise and said good-bye in English.

The two men went down the wooden steps to the gravel path and away from the overpowering presence of the trees to the road. They walked in silence until they came level with the small riverside café and there Chauvin stopped and said he insisted on treating his dear colleague from England to a drink. Over the drink, and the second one which Doherty bought, Chauvin explained the next steps he would order the Sûreté Urbaine—a first-class force—to take and why it was quite unnecessary to call in anyone from the regional branch of the Police Judiciaire.

★ ★ ★ ★

Doherty spent the next twenty-four hours waiting and wondering how to make time pass. Never a man for window-shopping, he soon exhausted any pleasure to be gained from staring at the shops and when he found a newsagent which had some old English paperbacks he bought three, even though they were titles he would normally never have read. At four o'clock in the afternoon, after drinking too many cups of coffee and eating too many *pâtisseries*, he looked round at the door to see Chauvin as the latter come into the lounge of the hotel.

They shook hands. Chauvin sat down, stared at the plate on which remained two *pâtisseries* and began to eat them, in rather an absentminded manner. He spoke between mouthfuls and occasionally during them. 'We have been active. Doctor Roget bought a house in Cagnes-sur-Mer and we are told it was not a cheap one. We have given orders for the body of Monsieur Decker to be... How d'you say?'

'Exhumed.'

'Exactly. We have spoken to many people who might be able to help and we have spoken to the undertakers.' Chauvin held the remaining half of the marron-filled coffee and chocolate-coated *pâtisserie* a bare inch from his mouth. 'They remember.'

'How much do they remember?'

'The funeral.'

'Why, after all this time, do they remember it?'

'Quite so. Why?' Chauvin took a large bite out of the *pâtisserie,* studied how little was left in his fingers and pushed the rest in.

Doherty impatiently watched the Frenchman's jaws move rhythmically up and down. 'Was something unusual?'

Chauvin swallowed. He wiped his mouth with the back of his hand. 'They remember because the body was so very... How d'you say?'

'I don't know.'

Chauvin pressed his nose with forefinger and thumb.

'Decomposed?'

'If that means it was becoming ripe, yes. It was June and hot, but even remembering that they say the body was not fresh. Yet the death certificate declares it was.'

'How long do they think the man could have been dead?'

'Five or six days. But we must recollect that they say this now, not then. Do you think he was poisoned and that was why things happened so quickly?'

Doherty's mind went back to the time he had stood in the hall of Hurstley Place and Mrs Decker had bemused him with a flood of words in order to keep him from asking the questions he wanted to ask her sons. She had told him how Hurstley Place had been saved to the Deckers because her husband had given the estate to a trust and had then died a mere two days outside the statutory five year period so that no death duties had to be paid.

'You have thought of something?' asked Chauvin.

'Possibly.'

'Will we find poison?'

'I don't think so. He died from natural causes and the death certificate will be right.'

'What a bore.'

Doherty wondered whether the other knew the meaning of that word. 'Could you do something more for me?'

'Certainly.'

'Find out if two men, whose photographs I'll have radioed over, visited the doctor's house in the south this summer and whether the doctor's bank accounts show any large deposit at the same time.'

'It shall be done.' Chauvin looked at the now empty *pâtisserie* plate. He sighed.

★ ★ ★ ★

Wade drove up to Hurstley Place at ten o'clock Thursday morning. He parked the Dodge shooting-brake in front of the steps and when he climbed out of it he looked rather like a small pea escaping from a very large pod.

He walked between the pillars of the porch and knocked on the front door. Every time he looked at this vast mansion, he was surprised that the family should continue to live in it: the most elementary application of common sense to economics must tell them that in this day and age it was ridiculous to pay for the upkeep of such a place. Waste hurt him. He had once tried to explain to Fawcett Decker the advantages in a move: Fawcett Decker had been exceptionally rude.

The door was opened by the Wop butler. Wade disliked all foreigners, especially ones who stood taller than himself. He was shown into the study and whilst on his own he stared at the illuminated addresses and thought how absurd they were.

Julian came into the room. 'Good morning.'

'It's nice of you to see me like this.' Wade wasted no more time on conventional pleasantries. He acknowledged the fact that the Deckers and the Wades of the world were poles apart and that there was nothing to be gained from trying to ignore this fact. 'I've come about the shoot, like.'

Julian sat down behind his desk and offerered cigarettes, which were refused. He suggested Wade should sit down, but Wade preferred to remain standing.

'With Bill and Joe dead,' said Wade, 'there's only me and Charlie left. Bill used to take the four guns so I was wondering what's the arrangement for next season?'

'I hadn't got around to thinking about it.'

'Could you have a think now?'

'I'm sorry, but there's a hell of a lot else...'

'I'm not one for beating about the bush. With Bill dead, I'm ready and willing to take over the guns. Two thousand five or six hundred quid, is it?'

'The cost of the shoot is rising pretty steeply.'

'That's all right by me. Give or take a few hundred quid and you won't find me squealing. I'd like them four guns.'

'What about Mr Cranleigh?'

'You can leave the details to me.'

Julian studied Wade. Of the four, he had always disliked Wade the least. Wade never sought, or pretended, to be other than what he was and he, Julian had never agreed that under Wade's manners lay a sneering sarcasm. 'I'll give you first refusal.'

'I came hoping for better than that.'

'If there's a shoot next year, you'll have first refusal.'

'You're surely not thinking of closing down?'

'I don't know what's going to happen,' replied Julian wearily.

Wade's cold blue eyes studied Julian's face. 'It's kind of you to see me,' he said finally, in his unemotional voice.

Wade left and Julian followed him out into the hall. After saying good-bye, he watched Wade cross the porch and step down to his car, in which he was engulfed. As the shooting-brake drove out of the garden and across the cattle-grid, another car slowed down until the way was clear and then came round the lawn. Julian recognised his cousin's Morris.

Henry Decker came into the house. 'I've a job in the next village for a client with a lot of money and not much taste so I thought I'd pop in and see how things are.'

'Come along and see Mother. She's polishing the silver and provided you don't try to tell her that there are at least a dozen better ways of polishing silver to the one she's using, she'll be very glad to see you. How's Clara?'

'Not too well. This damp weather upsets her so much.'

'I'm sorry to hear that.'

'I know. Tell me, wasn't that old Wade who passed me?'

'It was. He came to try to take over the guns for next season.'

'Did he? I suppose with Rafferty dead, he's all right in business and can afford a few of the "simple luxuries" of life. It's amazing how successful you can be these days provided you're totally devoid of a conscience.'

They walked through to the dining-room. One end of the table was covered with green baize and on this was all the silver that Lydia was cleaning.

She looked up. 'Hallo, Henry. I was saying only yesterday that you and Clara simply must come and have dinner soon. It's ages since we last saw her. Is she well?'

'She's not too bright, I'm afraid. You know what this sort of weather does to her.'

'She doesn't have enough work to occupy her mind. I believe in the saying that work is the finest medicine of all. Now who first said that? I seem to remember it was an American. They're much more fond of work than the English, aren't they, but they get so interested in it they forget how to relax and either die from heart or ulcers. That's why it's become a matriarchal society, which isn't right. Women don't make good rulers and they get very stingy when they're rich. Personally, I can't see the point in working to make a lot of money if you're going to die young. It's like those people who win so much money on dog racing...'

'You mean football pools,' corrected Julian.

'Henry knows exactly what I mean. You're being very intolerant today. Henry, I have cleaned the silver with a mixture of jeweller's rouge and spirits ever since we lost our last butler... I think his name was McNaughton and he came from somewhere right up in Sutherland near one of the rivers we used to fish...but

Julian keeps on and on at me saying I ought to use some different and more modern method just because it's supposed to be quicker.'

Henry Decker smiled. 'Your method certainly brings the silver up well, even if it does take a little time,' he said diplomatically. He looked at the Queen Anne and Regency coffee-pots, tea-pots, milk jugs, queen's pattern cutlery, candelabra, dozen sets of silver plates, and the ornaments, and wondered what capital they represented.

'We'll have some coffee,' she said. 'Julian, where's Danelli?'

'I'm afraid I don't know.'

'Where's Fawcett?'

'Once again, I plead ignorance.'

'You really are most unhelpful.' She finished polishing a milk jug and set it down on her right, put the polishing rags in a neat pile and peeled off her gloves. 'I'll go and find Fawcett and tell Danelli to make some coffee.'

'I really can't stay...' began Henry Decker.

'Nonsense. You're not going to rush away when you've plenty of time to have coffee,' she answered, just before she hurried out of the room.

Henry Decker went to the table and picked up an eighteen inch long pheasant in silver. 'I'm no great lover of silver ornaments, but I've always thought how marvellously sculptured this piece is.'

'It's all right.'

'The plumage is so well delineated.'

'But what can you do with it?'

'I suppose it is a bit like that in this day and age.' He put down the pheasant. 'You sound a bit under the weather, Julian!'

'I'm not exactly on top of the world, certainly.'

'Don't let the two deaths get you down: they weren't anything to do with the organisation of the shoot. If the two men were so bloody gormless when it came to handling their guns, they were bound to blow their heads off sooner or later.'

'Can you still talk about accidents?'

'No one's proved the deaths were anything else, have they?'

'The police are doing their damnedest. They never stop asking questions. Haven't they been worrying you?'

'They came and had a word and took a couple of cartridges away, but that doesn't signify anything.'

'It signifies they're certain it was murder.'

Henry Decker shrugged his shoulders. 'I don't really think...'

'You reckon it was Fawcett,' said Julian harshly.

'That's absurd. Why in the name of hell should Fawcett murder them?'

'I don't know.'

'You're too close to it all, Julian, to see straight. If the police were stupid enough to suspect Fawcett of two murders they'd have asked him and you ten times as many questions as I bet they have done.'

And what would his cousin say, thought Julian, if he knew about the doctor in France who'd been bribed to fake the date of Fawcett John deCourcy Decker's death by five days?

★ ★ ★ ★

Doherty had been at home for only an hour when the front-door bell rang. He looked up from the TV at the clock on the mantelpiece and cursed. Tired out from the journey back from France, he had been hoping to get to bed early. Peggy stood up and left the room, ignoring his feeble assertions that he would go and see who the caller was.

Doherty heard a voice and recognised it as Detective Superintendent Quincy's. He cursed again. Quincy came into the room and on his round face was an angry expression. 'I've been waiting for a report. Waiting and nothing bloody well happening.'

Doherty stood up. 'I didn't get back until after seven, sir.'

'That's an hour ago.'

Peggy, who had been waiting outside the room, came in and so prevented the detective superintendent's saying what he had intended to. 'I'm sure you'd like some coffee to warm you up, Mr Quincy?'

He muttered something.

'Good. I'll go and put it on. I've been trying for the last hour to find out just what my husband's been up to,' she said lightly.

'And that's just what...' began Quincy.

'I'm quite certain he's got at least some wicked thoughts he ought to confess to.' With skill, she continued to talk in a bantering way until certain that Quincy's ill-temper had to some extent been blunted. Then, she left the room.

Quincy took off his overcoat and folded it over the back of a chair. 'I've been doing my nut, Sam.'

'Have you, sir?'

'Every half hour the A.C.C's been on to me with a shower of questions. What's your D.I doing in the Decker case? Is he doing anything? Is he asleep? What's he discovered in France? What's he doing now? Where is he now? Where, what, when, how, why? I tell you, Sam, I'm doing my nut.'

'I'm sorry I couldn't...'

'Did you get anywhere? Have you got the answers?'

'There was a P.M. The elder Decker did die from cerebral thrombosis and there's no question of any other cause. There is, however, cause to suspect the date of death on the certificate.'

'The date?'

'Officially, he died on the fifteenth of June. That's two days after the end of the five year period during which the estate had been in trust in order to escape death duties. If Decker had died more than two days before, the estate would have been liable for full death duties and that almost certainly would have meant the end of it.

The family would have had to sell up.'

'Good God!' muttered Quincy.

'My guess is that he died about two days before the day that marked the end of the five year period, or five days earlier than the certificate says. Julian Decker had been called to Plincennes where his father lay very ill in a hotel room. Both men knew only too well what a premature death would mean to the estate and to them the estate was greater than anything else. The doctor called in happened to be an elderly man, nearing retirement, with not much of a practice. He must have said the sick man must go into hospital. The Deckers refused. If the father were to die too soon, it would be catastrophe for the estate and rather than that they were prepared to do, or try, anything. Julian Decker must have explained the facts to the doctor and offered him a fortune for full co-operation if it became necessary. It did, and as a result the doctor was given the chance to go and live in the south, a chance that would never come a second time. He took it and hid the death for about five days.

'In July, the doctor suddenly became possessed of a great deal of money. He left Plincennes and went to live in the south. The Deckers did not have to sell Hurstley Place. Then, recently, Rafferty discovered a hint of what had happened. He detested the Deckers and saw this as a chance to throw some of their arrogance back in their faces. He and Abbotts went to Plincennes and down to Cagnes-sur-Mer, where they saw Doctor Roget just before he died. Roget's bank statements show that at this time he received a large sum of money. When they got back to this country, Rafferty knew that he could, at any moment, ruin the Decker estate. He cracked the whip and they had to prepare to dance. Just before they danced too long or too hard, they made one last effort to save everything. After all, Fawcett Decker had little to lose, but a great deal to protect.'

'What proof have you?'

'Proof?' Doherty shook his head. 'No legal proof.'

'But can you prove the date of old man Decker's death?'

'There's some circumstantial evidence. We know when the elder Decker was taken ill, when Julian Decker booked in at the hotel, when the doctor was called in, when the chambermaids were told on no account to enter the sick man's room and disturb him, when the undertakers were called in and what they thought, when the doctor received a large sum of money from nowhere... But the kind of proof that a court of law deals in? No. No, sir, at the moment's there's no proof.'

'Rafferty must have bribed the doctor to make a sworn statement. Find that.'

'We've already searched and found nothing. Now we'll search again, but...I don't think we'll find it.'

'And if you don't?'

'Then I suppose one result will be that the death duty bastards won't get their hooks into the estate.'

CHAPTER 12

Adams called the line of beaters to a halt and cursed them for getting out of order. One of the grammar school boys laughed, but immediately stopped when Adams walked over to him and cursed him, personally. After a while, Adams returned and gave the order to move forward once more and to keep a straight line or clear off home and watch the telly.

Several birds flushed on the right and two came over Adams's head. He looked up between the ash trees and watched them go. They were both cocks. By this stage of the season, the cocks had learnt what a shoot was all about and they tried either to scuttle round the beaters, with the cunning of a fox, or else to take wing early and escape out of the coverts at points where there were no guns. If too many had become wise, relatively few birds would go over the guns. This was King's Beat. If the birds were thin over the guns he'd break the bones of every flaming beater who didn't know that a straight line was one which didn't bend.

Two birds rose ahead and started to come back over him. He waved his hands and they turned, so that when they were clear of the trees they were heading for the guns. He heard two shots. That was better. With both previous shoots getting mucked up by the bloody fools killing themselves, this one had to be a success. It was useless having too many birds around near Xmas: they brought in the commercial poachers who'd beat up any keeper who dared to try to stop them. The modern poacher was a criminal, and a vicious one at that, not a hungry countryman.

His Labrador was worrying a large patch of bramble. He went over and hammered the near edge with his stick: there was a violent movement on the far side as a cock pheasant struggled to disentangle itself. The Labrador saw what was happening and dashed round and the pheasant, in one last frantic and desperate effort, broke free from the brambles and took to the air. A few yards farther on, there was a large flush of birds. Adams shouted to the line to hold, but to keep the sticks tapping. Three of the boys tried to play the fool, but another shout stopped them. Why didn't Jim keep some of them in order, he thought angrily?

The firing became heavy. The birds were going nicely over the guns and not all in one cloud. He wondered what the new guest was like and whether he knew which end of the gun the shot came out of. It was a tragedy that the blokes who could shoot hadn't any money and the blokes who had the money couldn't shoot. No matter how understanding the boss, a season's shooting was finally judged by the number of birds that had been killed and not by the number which had been shot at or got away.

As the flush was over, he called the line forward. They pushed their way slowly through the rhododendrons. Now, the birds were getting up in large numbers and the firing at times became like a roll of thunder. Adams relaxed slightly as he slowly admitted to himself that things weren't going too badly. Jim said he was a fool to worry himself sick but a real keeper had to worry.

They reached the last few yards and some boys in the centre forgot all orders and rushed forward to the flushing wire. This parted the remaining birds so that they fell out to the right and the left, instead of going straight ahead, thereby depriving the central guns of their final sport. Adams cursed, but without much venom since it was too late for too much harm to have been done.

He reached the flushing wire, lifted it, and stepped over. He pushed his way through the undergrowth and went round a couple of pollard willows which brought him to number 4 stand. The new man, Gross, was here. He'd been introduced to him after the first beat by Mr Julian. At first acquaintance, it seemed he wasn't a bad sort, a long way removed from the departed but unlamented Abbotts or Rafferty.

Gross spoke excitedly. 'I've never before seen birds like that, coming so evenly. They are wonderfully presented.'

'We did our best, sir,' replied Adams, with just a trace of arrogant pride in his voice. It was right and proper that the gun should acknowledge the quality of this shoot. 'How many did you get, sir?'

'I'm afraid some of them were too good for me.'

'They do come fairly high.' Adams looked at the dead birds which were in a small pile by the stick.

'I've twelve more to pick,' said Gross.

'Right, sir. I'll tell one of the pickers-up.'

Adams pushed his way through the bracken and the brambles to the ride. The new chap not only knew his manners enough to say what a bloody fine job the keepers had done, but also was a fair to reasonable shot. Adams felt almost cheerful.

He stood on the ride and looked to his right. With the wind as it was, numbers 2 and 3 would not have seen much of the shooting. One might have had some sport back on the flank, but after he'd come round the ride behind the other guns to take up position at his stand he would only have had the birds which broke across for Fage Wood.

He looked to his left and his attention was taken by something on the edge of the ride, sticking out from behind the trunk of an old oak tree that had fallen during the summer gale. He called his dog to him and went up the ride. As he neared this object, he identified it as the pushing bar at the back of the wheel-chair. An icy fear settled in his normally unimaginative mind. He ran to the trunk and then stopped suddenly, his left hip almost touching the wood. The wheel-chair was slewed half off the side. Mr Fawcett lay sprawled across the far arm. He had been shot.

CHAPTER 13

Williams made his final report on the following Tuesday. Doherty met him in the detective inspector's room in Ashford police station.

Williams took a cartridge case and a small plastic bag, filled with shot, from his suitcase and put them on the table by the desk. He looked across at Doherty. 'Have you seen the pathologist's report?'

'Yes, sir.'

'I agree with all the major findings. The dead man was shot at a range of about twelve feet and test firings with the suspect's gun confirm these figures.'

'Is there any possibility this time that it might have been an accident caused by the deceased's gun?'

'I've already said the range was twelve feet. Dammit, the dead man's gun was found just in front of the wheel-chair and in any case it was broken and unloaded.'

'I know, sir, but just for the records... When you say broken, you mean that the breach was in the open position?'

'Of course I mean just that.'

Doherty wrote in his note-book. Williams could huff and puff as much as he liked, but the evidence had to be noted down exactly, and comprehensively, for the lawyers.

Williams put his hands in his pockets and paced up and down the room. 'The gun was fired from a height of about four and a half feet, which is the height the muzzles of the gun would be at when at the shoulder of a man six foot tall and when aimed at the head of a man in a wheel-chair at a distance of twelve feet.'

Doherty made a rapid sketch and on this placed the figures he had just been given.

Williams came to a halt by the table and picked up the empty cartridge case. 'This is a sixteen bore cartridge which was loaded with number five shot. It was fired in an ejector gun. On the brass head are several distinctive marks caused by the ejector and by the firing-pin, marks which are exactly duplicated on test cartridges I have fired in the suspect's gun. I have prepared the usual comparison-micrometer photographs. There can be absolutely no doubt whatsoever that the cartridge case in question was fired from the suspect's gun.' He put the cartridge case back on the table and picked up the plastic bag of shot. 'Due to the centre of shot being fairly low and the spread being only a matter of an inch or so, we have been able to recover all the pellets. They form the load of a sixteen bore, number five, two and a half inch cartridge.'

Williams put the plastic bag of shot next to the cartridge on the table. 'One final point. As requested, immediately I had finished with the cartridge case, including the tests on the deposit, I sent it to the metallurgist, who returned it to me first thing this morning. Have you had his report yet?'

'Yes, sir. He telephoned it through. He can say quite positively that that cartridge case was not lying out in the open for more than twelve hours.'

Williams closed his suitcase. 'I'm handing these two exhibits over to you and I'll send the photographs along as soon as possible.' He picked up the suitcase. 'Will you be charging him with the other two killings as well?'

'That's one problem being left to the legal boys, sir.' He crossed to the desk and picked up the cartridge case and bag of shot. Automatically, he made certain the identifying labels were properly made out and attached.

'I hear you found the game counter as well?' asked Williams.

'It had fallen into the turn-up of Fawcett Decker's trousers.'

'Have you been able to check on the number of birds he'd shot up to that beat?'

'The figures we have match. In any case, he doesn't deny it's his counter. What he claims is that he lost it sometime and couldn't find it at the beginning of the day.'

'If he lost it then, how does he explain how the right number of birds shot by him appears on the counter?'

'He hasn't yet found a reasonable explanation for that one.'

Williams walked, with short jerky strides, over to the door. 'What's the estate worth?'

'They say it'll fetch half a million any day of the week.'

'I wonder how many of us would shoot our brothers for half a million?' Williams left the room and slammed the door shut behind himself.

Doherty stared at the far wall. Money,

in any form, always had tempted man and always would. But how many men were so rotten, so devoid of any degree of common humanity, that money would tempt them to commit fratricide? He felt deeply shocked that Julian Decker should have done this terrible thing: since he had met the Decker family his own feelings towards them had changed from amusement to respect. Now he found that he had been respecting a tradition that had grown rotten. Maybe all traditions became rotten after a while. He could have understood, and indeed had, the shooting of Rafferty and Abbotts—but there could be no understanding the crime of fratricide, committed for gain. Half a million pounds. Julian Decker had shot his brother for half a million pounds.

★ ★ ★ ★

Julian sat on the bunk in the cell. On the opposite wall, the whitewash was peeling: in one patch where it had not done so, some previous prisoner had written a virulently obscene description of the law.

He had been charged with the murder of Fawcett. It seemed an impossibility, until he looked round and saw the dirty walls, the dirty ceiling, and the steel door with its cyclopean peep-hole. How could any sane person believe he would murder Fawcett for the sake of inheriting the estate? How could any sane person believe he would so dishonour the family? He wasn't the first Decker to be imprisoned, but other Deckers had done no more than commit treason in the days when every man who supported the defeated claimant to the throne was guilty of treason. He was imprisoned for one of the filthiest of crimes.

He turned and hammered both fists against the wall of the cell at the back of the narrow bunk. Pain streaked up his arm and restored some sense to him. If he smashed his flesh against the wall for the next twenty-four hours, it would change nothing. He was charged with murder and he would be tried for murder: the murder of Fawcett Decker, his brother.

He remembered how, when she first heard what was happening, Barbara had stared at him with an expression of blank horror so great that it had robbed her of all her beauty: he hoped to God he never saw such an expression again.

He remembered the day of the shoot.

She had met him on the ride as she came down it to take up position for picking-up in the Larch Plantation. At the time, she had wondered what he was doing there as the birds were already coming over. He'd told her how he'd had a shot at a fox which he was fairly certain was seriously wounded and that he'd left the stand to try and find the fox and put it out of its misery. She had accepted the explanation without question. But when she heard about how Fawcett had been shot from the ride just for one fraction of a second there had been a doubt in her mind. That doubt had gone immediately. She trusted him. But if even she could momentarily doubt him, what were the jury going to do? Oh God! part of his mind cried, how had it happened? Suppose...suppose he were found guilty? Surely, despite her trust, she must eventually begin to believe the lie. It wouldn't be at the beginning, of course, but after a while the poison would act and the first doubt would creep into her mind. Doubt would multiply wildly, like a cancer. No matter how loyal she wanted to be, she could never stop that doubt from multiplying.

He hadn't killed Fawcett: nothing on

earth would have made him lift a hand against his brother. Yet the evidence was there. No matter how loudly he cried his innocence, he knew the evidence was there. Fawcett had been murdered. He had been shot with a sixteen bore cartridge that had been fired from the gun he, Julian, was using. It was impossible, yet the expert evidence was beyond contradiction. His lawyers had told him again and again that he could do himself nothing but harm by trying to disprove this evidence. Yet it had to be disproved because it was impossible. He hadn't fired a shot at the point where the empty cartridge case had been found.

It was like his game counter that the police had found. That was impossible. He had said again and again to the lawyers that it was impossible and they had sighed wearily. The counter was small, no bigger than the old fashioned type of bicycle milometer, with a plunger. He used it to record how many birds he had shot. That Saturday, he had searched for it in the gun-room and had failed to find it. Later, the police had discovered it in Fawcett's turn-up and it had recorded 36. The police had been clever. At first, they had merely asked him how many birds he had shot up to the beginning of King's Beat. He had told them, 33. He'd also said that because he'd lost the counter, he'd had to keep a mental count. Then they asked him, so casually, about the counter. He told them that at the end of each shooting day he entered the number it recorded in his game-book, after which he reset the counter to zero. Did he always re-set the counter to zero? Always, he answered. And how many birds had he shot the previous shoot? 51. Only later did he discover how self-incriminating his answers had been. The police went on to question the other guns to find out how many birds they'd shot: no one had shot more than 20.

They claimed he'd shot Fawcett because Fawcett was the elder brother, due to inherit the estate under trust. But Fawcett had already agreed that he would never claim the estate when the day came for him to make the election: he knew he must die before long, when the unwanted miracle of his continued living came to an end. Nothing would ever lead him to accept the estate since within days, weeks, or months, he must die and death duties would strip the estate and ruin it. When he refused the inheritance, it would come to Julian which was the best, indeed only, solution to ensure the continuation of Hurstley Place. But there was no proof of this other than the word of the family. There had never been any need for documents, not between members of the Decker family.

His lawyers had explained to him that as he had been charged only with the murder of Fawcett there was an obvious defence, if true, open to him. He could admit he had shot Fawcett, but claim the shooting was an accident. Fawcett had been number 1 gun so that he started up on the right flank of the guns, had come down to the ride keeping level with the beaters, and had then come along the ride towards number 1 stand. Julian had shot at the fox and had gone to the ride to try to find the wounded animal to put it out of its misery. It was obvious, said the lawyers, how so tragic an accident could occur. When he reached the ride, he saw Fawcett in his wheel-chair, which had just slid off the ride because the wet ground was so slippery. Julian hurried to give assistance and in his hurry had stumbled when, by dreadful mischance, his finger was round the trigger. The gun had gone off and killed his brother. He had not admitted this before because he had been too ashamed. Of course, the lawyers had gone on to say, such a defence of accident was very much a double-edged weapon. The plea would immediately allow the prosecution to introduce the evidence of the other two deaths. Similar occurrences to that charged were not normally admissible evidence, but they became so if necessary to rebut a plea of accident. The jury, went on the lawyers with massive understatement, would not be inclined to give much weight to the plea of accident when they were presented with the evidence also of the deaths of Abbotts and Rafferty. Juries were usually rather stupid, but even the most stupid jury would not believe in three similar accidents. Nevertheless, the lawyers had said in ponderous manner, if the death of Fawcett was an accident, obviously Julian must so testify. And may the Lord have mercy on your soul, he had almost heard them add.

He had told them he knew nothing at all about the death of Fawcett. The Q.C had looked aggrieved, upset anyone should treat him as a fool. The junior had whispered something to the solicitor, who had looked quickly at Julian and then shaken his head with much force.

Julian stood up and paced the cell. Four paces this way, four paces that: four paces this way, four paces that. There was a tempest raging in his mind. He thought of his utter innocence and he thought of Barbara. He remembered her face, radiant, on the day of their engagement: he remembered it when she learned he was suspected of Fawcett's murder. His mind seemed to be about to explode from its load of self-pity, desperation, fear, and desolation. Once again, he wanted to hammer at the walls with his fists, in the childish belief that they must come tumbling down before his innocence. But another part of his mind mocked him. In the modern world, of what value was mere innocence?

CHAPTER 14

Avonley Assize Court was part of the borough council buildings, an area of unrelieved ugliness. The courtroom had a very high ceiling with elaborately moulded plaster work, which was held to be responsible for the bad acoustics. Lawyers on the circuit had many apocryphal stories of prisoners being convicted of crimes they hadn't been charged with because neither judge nor jury had been able to hear a word that was said.

Mr Justice Arneld wore horn-rimmed glasses and had a round face with lines about his mouth that suggested he was about to smile: this was usually a false suggestion. When evidence of the finding of the body was over, the judge spoke to the clerk of the court, who stood up on his chair so that his head reached the level of the top of the desk on the dais. They spoke for a few moments before the clerk resumed his seat. 'Yes, Mr Calaghan,' said the judge to prosecuting counsel.

Calaghan, who had been speaking to his instructing solicitor, turned round, looked down at his notes and called for the next witness, the police doctor. Whilst the doctor was crossing to the witness-box, Calaghan rearranged his papers. He poured some water into a glass and drank as the doctor took the oath.

The witness gave his evidence with the assurance of someone who was often in the witness-box. He testified that he had been called to woods on the Hurstley Place estate and there had seen the body of Fawcett Decker in a wheel-chair. A plan of the area was referred to and he confirmed the spot at which the wheel-chair had been. He testified he had made a superficial examination of the dead man, finding an extensive entry wound, but not exit wound. There had been no marginal burning or tattooing around the wound. There were some marginal pellet holes, proof that the fatal gun had been fired from a distance, but he was not qualified to say what that distance was.

Welter, defending silk, cross-examined very briefly. 'Doctor, did you undertake any experiments to ascertain the direction from which the gun had been fired?'

'I did not.'

'Or the height at which the muzzles were?'

'No.'

Welter sat down and watched the doctor leave the box. He thought glumly how it was one thing to have some facts favourable to the defence and so be able to fight, but that it was quite another to be left with nothing in one's favour so that the fight was lost before it had even started. Julian Decker must be a fool. Why, after two perfect murders, did he leave enough evidence around at the third one to convict himself twice over? Had he suddenly panicked? It seemed the most likely explanation. In which case, it was the appearance of Miss Harmsworth that had caused him to panic. She had come along the ride just after he had fired the gun and he had had to move quickly to prevent her attention being drawn to the body in the wheel-chair, almost hidden by the crashed oak tree. How the hell could he, Welter, begin to present a defence? A straight denial of everything was doomed to failure: yet to plead accident was to commit forensic suicide when such defence immediately allowed the prosecution to introduce the details of the other two killings. Not, of course, that such details weren't already in the minds of the jury. With the news coverage that had been given those details, there could hardly be anyone in the British Isles who hadn't heard or read about them.

Two witnesses gave formal evidence and he declined to cross-examine. Cortelan, his instructing solicitor, turned and tried to attract his attention, but he shook his head. Cortelan was one of the world's worst worriers and right now he, Welter, had enough worries of his own.

The Home Office pathologist was called. Welter reached under his wig and scratched the back of his head. The only course open to him here was to try and get the admission that this could have been an accidental shooting, without actually putting such a proposition. Then the groundwork would be there should Decker suddenly decide even as late as this to take the risk and call it an accident.

Welter stood up to cross-examine. He studied the witness. Here was a man who was completely confident of himself, a confidence well placed. There would be nothing but harm to be gained from challenging him on most of the points: more especially, thought Welter angrily, as there wasn't a scrap of evidence to back up such a challenge. 'You say you recovered all the shot?'

'That is right.'

'Can you swear you did not miss one single pellet?'

'I've already testified that I cannot swear

to have regained every last one, but I am prepared to state that the chance of having missed more than four or five is exceedingly remote.'

'You can say that the path of the shot is roughly on a level?'

'Yes.'

'Does this preclude any position other than that the gun was held parallel to the ground?'

'The alternatives are, as I have tried to explain, that the deceased's head was inclined upwards or downwards and that the muzzles of the gun were higher or lower than four feet above the ground.'

'Are you calling these unlikely possibilities?'

'At the distance at which the shot was fired, even so small an angle as five degrees of inclination of the head means a difference in height of the muzzles of the gun of about one foot.'

'If the gun were held at the trail there would be at least two feet difference in height compared to the gun held at the shoulder?'

'If the gun were held at the trail with the muzzles tilting upwards to give the necessary angle of shot, the difference in height would be about twenty-four inches, yes.'

'And the head of the deceased would have to be tilted downwards about ten degrees?'

'That is so.'

'Would you think this was a possible position?'

'It is possible,' replied the doctor, in a neutral tone of voice.

Welter sat down. Temporarily, he had planted in the minds of the jury the picture of the man carrying the gun at the trail, But, logic insisted on telling him, for how long would that picture last when the prosecution proved that Decker was a fanatic on safe gun handling and had never, never carried his gun in so inherently a dangerous position as the trail? Further, if just for once he had done so, how or why did his finger happen to be resting on the for'd trigger?

Williams was called to the witness-box. He gave his evidence clearly and concisely. The deceased had been shot with a shotgun, at a range of about twelve feet. Williams had been given the shot which was removed from the head of the deceased and it consisted of 203 number

5 shot pellets, weighing almost 15/16ths of an ounce. This was the standard charge for a 2½" 16 bore cartridge. He had been handed an empty 2½" 16 bore cartridge case and had examined it. On the brass base were certain marks caused by the ejector and the striking-pin: such marks were always unique, being particular to one gun. He had been handed a gun with which he had carried out test firings. He had compared cartridges fired from the test gun with the control cartridge case and the marks on the bases were exactly similar proving beyond any doubt that that gun had fired the control cartridge.

Prosecuting counsel studied the jury's face and saw on none of them the kind of baffled or blank expression that would show they had failed to understand the purport or importance of the evidence just given. He half turned and spoke to the witness once more. 'I want you to look at a gun. Exhibit number sixteen, please.'

The usher picked up a shotgun from the table in front of the desk at which the clerk of the court and the shorthand writer sat. He carried the shotgun across to Williams.

Williams took the gun, broke it, and

checked it was unloaded before examining it.

'Is that the test gun?'

'It is.'

'How do you identify it?'

'It is a Holland best gun. The number of it, just beyond the trigger guard, is one two nine eight.'

Calaghan addressed the Bench. 'It will be proved, my lord, that this is the gun the accused was using on the day in question.'

In the dock, Julian stared at his gun. They were proving this was the murder weapon, yet it had never fired the shot that killed Fawcett. Why wasn't his counsel fighting every inch of the way? It was impossible that a newly-fired cartridge, fired from his gun, had been at the point where the police claimed to have found it. Why wasn't his counsel calling the police liars?

Welter stood up to cross-examine. Williams often appeared as an expert witness in shooting cases and the public were beginning to think of him as a man so expert in his own sphere he could never be wrong in it. That was a very dangerous thing, because juries began to place uncritical and total reliance in his evidence. Yet, in this case, why should they do otherwise? 'Mr Williams, I have listened very carefully to your evidence but I confess that I still do not understand how you can be so sure that the empty cartridge case, exhibit number fifteen, was the cartridge that killed the deceased?'

'I have not said that it was.'

'I thought you were implying this?'

'I have been implying nothing. I have simply given the facts.'

Welter spoke blandly, with just a trace of surprise in his voice. 'In that case, we really must look at the facts again to see we are not misleading ourselves. You were given the empty cartridge case and a gun. You can tell us that, beyond any shadow of doubt, that gun fired that cartridge?'

'I have already said so.'

'Indeed. You have even produced some excellent photographs to prove your point.'

Williams disdained to comment.

'You also conducted certain experiments, independently of the metallurgist, to determine whether the control cartridge had been recently fired?'

'Yes.'

'And you came to the conclusion, after chemical tests on the deposit left inside the case, that it had been fired within the twenty-four hours previous to your tests?'

'Yes.'

'But you can't tell us at what precise hour of those twenty-four it was fired?'

'Of course not.'

'And you cannot tell us at what the cartridge was fired?'

The judge, testily, intervened. 'Mr Welter, this witness has done no more than testify that the control cartridge case, found on the ride near the body, was fired by the accused's gun and fired within the previous twenty-four hours to his examination on it.'

'Quite so, my lord.'

'Then I fail to see any point to your cross-examination.'

'Very well, my lord, if you insist,' said Welter in an angry tone of voice, as if he had just been prevented from making some very damaging point. He sat down.

Calaghan did not re-examine—an open, but silent, declaration that he believed Welter's cross-examination to have achieved nothing. He called the metallurgist. The witness gave evidence that from the condition of the brass cap of the control cartridge it had been clear the cartridge had not lain out in the open all Friday night when it had rained heavily.

'No questions,' said Welter.

Adams was called. In the witness-box, dressed in a tweed shooting-suit that did not fit, he looked as he felt, a fish out of water.

'You are head gamekeeper on the estate?' asked Calaghan, once the preliminary question had been put.

'Yes, sir.'

'For how long?'

'Over thirty years.'

'Obviously, then, you know the estate very well?'

'I reckon to.'

'Is it correct that you look after certain beats and your under-keeper looks after others?'

'That's right, sir.'

'Which of you two is in charge of King's Beat?'

'Me.'

'Will you tell us what work this entails on a shooting day?'

'I...I don't quite understand.'

'I'm sorry. I'll put it another way. When King's Beat is being shot, what work do you have to do in or around the beat on the morning of the shoot and before the shooting starts?'

'I feed, natural like, prepare the flushing wire, put up them numbers, and make certain all is well. Then I goes back to my cottage for a bite of something if there's time and then out with the beaters, beating-in.'

'Out on the beat you feed the pheasants and so on, and put up the numbers. What exactly does that mean?'

Adams was bewildered and unable to understand the need for any further explanation. 'Put 'em on the sticks.'

The judge intervened. 'I am afraid we need a better explanation than that. Mr Calaghan, for those of us who are not conversant with the mechanics of a day's shooting.'

Calaghan prompted the witness. 'You put up a mark where the gun is to stand?'

'I puts the numbers in sticks where each gun stands. Then if Mr Julian isn't there to tell 'em, the guns can find where to go.' As he spoke Julian's name, Adams looked at the desk. He immediately looked away again.

'Do you have a routine for putting up the numbers at King's Beat?'

'I walks down the ride...'

'Just a moment. Will you look at the plan. Usher, give Mr Adams the plan, exhibit number one.' Calaghan waited until it had been handed to Adams. 'When you talk about the ride, do you mean the ride which runs in front of the Larch Plantation?'

'Yes, sir.'

'Right. Now you walk down that. What happens as you go down?'

'When I'm level with each stand I goes up to it and puts the number in a stick.'

'Did you do this on the Saturday in question?'

'Yes, sir.'

Calaghan put one foot on the empty seat next to his and rested his left elbow on his knee. 'I suppose that whenever you're walking through the woods you must always be on the lookout for anything of interest?'

'I am that.'

'What sort of thing would interest you?'

'Anything to do with poaching or if the stoats and weasels be strong. Maybe a fox's taken a bird.'

'What kind of signs do poachers usually leave?'

'Depends on how they poaches. Some use two twos or a shotgun and then there's still some use burning sulphur, raisins and fish hooks, or a noose on a stick. There's more ways than there is of killing a cat.'

'What happens when they use guns? How d'you know they have?'

'By feathers and blood.'

'Anything else?'

'There's the cartridge cases, of course.'

'I see. Would you notice an empty cartridge case on a ride if you hadn't seen it there before?'

'Of course I would.' Adams spoke scornfully.

'Then did you see an empty cartridge case on this ride below King's Beat, near the fallen oak tree, on Saturday, December the fourth?'

It was obvious that, too late, Adams realised the reason for the questions that he had considered ridiculous. He stared at counsel with hatred.

'Did you notice a cartridge case?'

'I...I wasn't rightly looking.'

'Have you not just assured us that you could never ever overlook such an object?'

Welter, not bothering to stand, spoke loudly. 'Are you applying to treat this witness as hostile?'

Calaghan half turned. 'I wouldn't call him hostile, merely temporarily obstructive.'

The judge spoke to the witness. 'Did you see an empty cartridge case in the ride, near the spot on the plan marked "cartridge"?'

Adams looked down at the plan that he still held. His grizzled face expressed the worried turmoil in his mind. A genuine love for the family he had served for so many years battled with his dread of lying to the law.

'You will answer,' snapped the judge.

'Well I...I didn't, but that don't mean there wasn't one there.'

Calaghan took up the questioning. 'Are you now trying to reverse your previous evidence and say that you might have missed an empty cartridge case lying out in the ride?'

'I might've done.'

'You might have done,' repeated Calaghan, with heavy emphasis on the word 'might.' 'One last point. Did any other part of the shoot that day take place near King's Beat?'

'No.'

'And did you hear any shots other than the shots you expected to hear from the guns in position?'

'No.'

Welter cross-examined. He smiled and spoke in his friendliest voice. 'Mr Adams, please don't let yourself be bullied into saying something which you don't mean.'

'By the same token,' interrupted the judge, 'the witness will not allow himself to be led into inaccuracies by anything you may say.'

'Quite so, my lord.' Welter turned back. 'Mr Adams, on a shooting day you must be a very busy man?'

'Maybe,' answered Adams, who was determined not to make any more admissions to anyone.

'And since the success, or otherwise, of the day's shooting falls on your shoulders you have a very great deal to think about.'

'Maybe.'

'You must, indeed, have so much to think about that your mind cannot at all times be fully focused on what it is that you are doing at some particular moment? When you were walking down the ride in question, you were probably deep in thought about all the thousand and one things pertaining to the shoot?'

Calaghan stood up. 'Perhaps my learned friend would prefer that he should give the evidence?'

'Without a doubt,' replied the judge, 'but such opportunity will not be offered him in my court. Mr Welter, you will leave the witness to give the evidence.'

'But of course, my lord, since nothing would better suit my case.' Welter continued his cross-examination. 'On Saturday the fourth of December you were holding one of your big shoots, were you not?'

'That's right.'

'Does such a shoot require more planning than a smaller day would?'

Adams hesitated.

'Let me put it another way. Would you describe yourself as concerned with more details on a big day than on a small day?'

'Maybe.'

Welter looked at the jury. 'Then in such circumstances it is easy to see how preoccupied you must have been.' He sat down.

Calaghan re-examined very briefly. 'Do you agree with what you said earlier? That whenever you are in the woods you are automatically on the lookout for signs of poaching?'

'Well, I...'

'Are empty cartridge cases one such sign?'

'Yes.'

'Did you walk along this ride and past the spot where we know this empty cartridge case was found before the shoot began?'

'I...'

'Did you?'

'Yes,' muttered Adams.

'Did you see an empty cartridge case there?'

'No.'

'Thank you. That is all.'

Adams slowly turned and left the box. He looked at the dock and there was an expression of worried shame on his face. For the first time in over thirty years, he had betrayed the Decker family.

'The court will adjourn for lunch,' the judge said. He stood up, returned counsels' bows, and left.

★ ★ ★ ★

Immediately he was outside the court, Calaghan spoke to his instructing solicitor and asked him to find Detective Inspector Doherty. The solicitor left and returned within the minute with Doherty.

Calaghan led the way to a corner of the entrance hall. 'I wanted a quick word with you, Inspector.' He took off his wig and ran his fingers through his hair.

'Yes, sir?'

'The other side has laid a little of the groundwork for a defence of accident although obviously they can't yet make up their minds whether to use it. We've got to be prepared to meet such a defence and I'm just a little worried about the evidence concerning the death of the elder Fawcett Decker.' He took a cigarette case from his pocket and all three men smoked. 'We've some circumstantial evidence to show that the father died just before the five year period was up and that Julian Decker bribed the French doctor to give the wrong date of death, but we've not the final proof, the kind of proof the jury will want. I suppose you haven't turned up anything in the last day, or two?'

'I'm afraid not, sir. We've checked every lead we have, without luck.'

'The doctor must have given Rafferty a sworn statement—there's no other reasonable explanation for that large payment into his bank immediately after Rafferty's visit to him in the south of France this year.'

'Yes, sir, but we haven't found any such statement.'

Calaghan tapped his chin with his brief. He turned to his solicitor. 'It's a weakness, but I don't suppose we need worry about it very much.'

'If the other side does plead accident and you present them with the known facts of the father's death and Rafferty's and Abbotts's deaths, they'll draw the right inference quickly enough, whether or not the statement's found.'

'I'm inclined to agree with you.' Calaghan lowered his brief and held it under his arm. 'Although it's nothing to do with the case I've been thinking about the question of the date of death in connection with the liability for death duties. On the available evidence it's obvious what happened, but I doubt very much there's even the proof for the government to be able to levy the death duties that would have been payable on the father's death.'

'That's what I thought, sir,' said Doherty.

Calaghan looked at the detective. 'The possibility doesn't unduly worry you?'

'No, sir. I never liked death duties even though they'll not worry my estate.'

'Three men have been murdered because of them.'

'If the date of the father's death was hushed up, it was done before the murders, sir.'

'That's an Irish way of looking at things.'

'I was born an Irishman, sir.'

Calaghan smiled.

★ ★ ★ ★

Julian was brought his lunch on a tray. After the warder had left and shut and locked the cell door, Julian removed the covers from the dishes. There was steak, fried potatoes, peas, roll and butter, and trifle and cream. As a person not yet convicted, he was allowed to buy, or have bought for him, food cooked by outside caterers. He cut through the steak. In the centre the meat was red which was how he liked it, yet he had never less wanted to eat. The last time he remembered having eaten steak had been at the Newingreen Motel, when he was with Barbara. Afterwards, they had driven on to Hythe and along the coast road to Greatstone and Dungeness. A mile or so before Dungeness, they had stopped the car and walked across the shingle, past the drawn-up fishing boats, down to the sand. The tide had been out and, slightly formless in the soft moonlight, the sand had seemed to stretch for hundreds of yards. The sea was alive with glitter. He remembered the large ship, ablaze with lights, sailing up the Channel. Both he and Barbara had had the same thought: a honeymoon at sea...

He looked round the cell. A honeymoon at sea! What a hell of a bloody thing to think of in a dirty, stinking cell. Bitterly, he pushed the tray of food along the bunk. He could not eat, not when his mind was so savagely torturing his body.

CHAPTER 15

Danelli said he would carry the dish, but Lydia Decker ignored him and took it into the dining-room. She put the dish with the others on the serving table and helped herself to meat, potatoes, and vegetables. She sat down at the head of the table. She was alone, now, one woman at a table which could seat twenty-four. She was the only Decker left in the mansion of thirty-one bedrooms. She had been at the funeral of her husband and of one of her sons, and now her remaining son was on trial for fratricide. Another woman would have been crushed by the weight of the tragedies, but she still had one great thing left to help her retain her courage and sanity. She had Hurstley Place. Here, the Deckers lived on. In this dining-room, George the Fourth, when Prince Regent had dined and wined so well that three men had had to escort him to bed.

Here, Fawcett Brett Decker had returned from the Battle of Waterloo to find his wife had taken very deeply to religion: the parson left the parish that same day. Here, Elizabeth Decker had been married to one of the Dukes of Weimar, very soon to return from that country because she found the inhabitants 'barbarous and lacking the graces of a polite society.' And here she, Lydia Charlotte Decker, waited until it was time to go to the court where they were trying the sole surviving male Decker of the direct line.

She heard the front door knocker sound as she served herself. As she sat down, Barbara came into the room. Lydia saw in her face grief as great as her own. She stood up, went over to Barbara, and put an arm round her shoulders.

Barbara wept, with a quiet but bitter passion. After a while, she gained some control over her emotions. She wiped the tears from her eyes and cheeks with a handkerchief.

'Come and sit down,' said Lydia. She led Barbara to the table and then went across to the small table in the corner of the room where she poured out a whisky. Barbara tried to refuse the drink, but could not outlast the elder woman's insistence that she should drink it.

'I've had to wait all morning,' said Barbara, in a toneless voice. 'Wait outside the courtroom, knowing he's inside and being tried. I heard two policemen talking. They said he hadn't a dog's chance in hell: they said that any man who killed his brother deserved everything that was coming to him. I shouted at them and they stared at me as if I was mad. Lydia, I've got to go back there and wait all afternoon and when they call me inside they're going to ask me if I saw him on the ride. I won't tell them...I won't.'

'You will have to,' replied Lydia quietly.

'I'll lie.'

'They'll show you're lying and that will do a great deal of harm.'

'Don't you care what happens to him?'

'I care.'

'Maybe you think he shot Fawcett. Do you think he's a murderer?'

'Finish your drink and then have something to eat.'

'I can't eat anything.'

'You must do.'

'You're so damned cold blooded,' shouted Barbara.

Lydia shivered. She went across to the serving table and put meat and vegetables on the second plate there: the second plate Danelli had laid, as if to pretend there would be two Deckers to lunch, not just one.

When she returned to the table and placed the plate in front of Barbara, Barbara spoke.

'Please, I'm sorry. I...I don't know what I'm saying.'

Lydia touched her briefly before she sat down. 'Grief is something I've had to learn to live with ever since the day Fawcett was not very well and we asked our doctor to examine him. I've had to learn to treat grief as something that is completely natural and to be expected.'

'But...but suppose they find him guilty?'

'We must pray they do not.'

'I can't pray. How can I begin to pray when this has happend to him?'

'It's worth trying, Barbara. Sometimes prayer has helped me, sometimes it's seemed to mock me. When my husband died, it did both things at once.' Lydia watched Barbara finish her drink. 'Eat as much as you can, now.'

Around and above them, Hurstley Place stood square to the rising wind, unaffected by any storm.

★ ★ ★ ★

The trial resumed at five minutes past two. The police constable who found the game counter was called and gave his evidence. Henry Decker, Cranleigh, Wade, Lenton, and Gross then went in turn into the witness-box, were questioned on what size gun and cartridges they had been using, and how many birds they had shot up to the beginning of King's Beat. Welter, almost halfheartedly, tried to prove that the numbers they gave could only be approximate since none of them had visibly recorded his bag in any way, but this helped the defence not at all. Even allowing a considerable margin of error, it was clear that none of them had shot more than twenty birds. Julian Decker had told the police that up to the beginning of this beat he had shot thirty-three birds and that out of the early birds to come over, before he went to the ride to look for the fox, he had shot three more. That gave the figure of thirty-six that had been on the game counter found in Fawcett's turn-up. That figure could not be Fawcett's total of kills because, by taking all known figures from the total bag, it was obvious that his share to the time of his death could not be more than seventeen.

Calaghan was a prosecuting counsel who tried to make as certain as was ethically possible that the defence was not given the slightest chance. Therefore, he had advised that the number of birds Julian had shot on November the twentieth must be proved, to refute any possible defence allegation that this was the number on the game counter. Detective Constable Pawley was called.

'Did you go to Hurstley Place after the accused had been taken into custody to make certain inquiries?'

'Yes, sir.'

'What were those inquiries?'

In the witness-box, Pawley was almost deferential. Although he would not have admitted it, he was almost scared by the outward majesty of the law and the courts. 'I went to Hurstley Place, sir, and asked for Mr Julian Decker's game-book.'

'Whom did you ask?'

'The butler sir. His name is Danelli.'

'Did he give it to you?'

'At first he said he couldn't, but when

I explained I must have it he went away and got it for me.'

'Is this the game-book he gave you...? Usher, will you pass exhibit number twenty-seven to the witness, please.' Calaghan addressed the judge. 'My lord, photostat copies of the relevant page have been prepared for your lordship and the jury.'

'Very well.'

The witness identified the book and opened it. Calaghan waited whilst the photostat copies were handed around, then questioned the witness once more. 'Will you look at the last entry on page one hundred and four.'

'I am, sir.'

'What is the date?'

'November the twentieth, sir.'

'Will you read out the figures given there.'

'Pheasants fifty-one, duck nine, woodcock one, hares one, various seven, sir.'

'Does that make a grand total of sixty-nine?'

'Yes, sir.'

'If the accused were recording on his counter just the number of pheasants shot, then, the figure would be fifty-one: if everything, sixty-nine. Thank you.'

Welter stood up. So far, tactics had dictated that he did not fight too belligerently. To attack a witness solely for the sake of attacking was wrong tactics, employed only by the rawest of barristers: but at some stage or other of a trial a counsel had, if possible, to attack a witness of the other side because juries would only believe a counsel who appeared to believe in his client. This apparent paradox was more often than not resolved by defence counsel by attacking a police witness. Police witnesses were fair game, in season throughout the seasons, and an attack on them even when totally abortive need not, if carefully handled, rebound disastrously on the defence. It was Pawley's bad luck that he was, so far as Welter was concerned, the right person at the right place at the right time.

Welter stared at Pawley with an obvious dislike. 'What were your orders?' he finally demanded.

'My orders, sir?'

'That's what I asked.'

'I'm sorry, but I don't understand, sir.'

'Then I shall have to put it more simply.' The expression on Welter's face suggested the witness was being deliberately obstructive. 'Why did you go to Hurstley Place?'

'To obtain the game-book, sir.'

'Yes, yes, we've heard that. But did you go on your own account or because you were given order to do so?'

'I was given orders, sir.'

'Were you given any unusual instructions on how to ask for the game-book?'

'No, sir.'

'You were to conduct yourself as you normally do?'

'Of course, sir.'

'Constable, there is no "of course" about it.' Welter was silent for a few seconds, then he said: 'What did you say when you spoke to the butler?'

'I asked him for the game register belonging to Mr Julian Decker.'

'What do you mean by the word "ask"?'

'What do I mean?'

'Surely that question is simply enough phrased for you to understand?'

'But I don't...'

Welter leaned forward and his voice rose slightly. 'Would it be correct to say that by "ask" you mean threaten?'

'Certainly not, sir.'

'Let's examine the facts.' Welter picked

up a sheet of paper and studied it. 'Do you remember your first words to the butler?'

'Not exactly, sir, but I just introduced myself.'

'And then?'

'I asked for the game register.'

'Asked for it or demanded it?'

'Asked for it, sir.'

'Were you given it at this point?'

'No, sir. He told me he couldn't.'

'But you did not accept his refusal?'

'Well, I couldn't.'

'You couldn't?' repeated Welter heavily. 'Did you say to Mr Danelli you must have the game register or there would be trouble?'

'Not like that sir. I didn't suggest...'

'I shall tell you what you suggested. Mr Danelli is an Italian who, although he has worked in this country for several years, has an exaggerated respect for the police and their powers. Are you aware that your threats terrified him, Constable?'

'That's not true.'

'You terrified him. All he was doing was legitimately to try to defend the interests of the family for whom he worked and as a direct result he was threatened by you if he refused to hand over the game register.'

'But I didn't threaten him...'

'Did you or did you not tell him he could be in trouble if he continued to refuse to let you have the game register?'

'I...I may have said something like that, but it wasn't a threat.'

'Will you try to explain to the jury how you can threaten a man with trouble and yet not threaten him? Will you explain to the jury how you can browbeat a foreigner, unaware of the restrictions wisely placed on police action in this country, and yet not threaten him?'

'I keep telling you, I didn't threaten him.'

'You keep telling me that, Constable, but, to be quite frank, I don't believe you. I imagine that the jury will similarly disbelieve you.'

Pawley, not without reason, was stupid enough to lose his temper. 'I didn't threaten him. I didn't threaten him, whatever the old fool says. I didn't hit him, or beat him...'

Welter broke in. 'You didn't actually hit or beat him, so you can stand there and proudly claim you used no threats? We all take careful note of your standards of behaviour.' Welter sat down.

'That's all,' said Calaghan.

Pawley stared with hatred at prosecuting counsel. Why wasn't the bloody fool re-examining to show that defence counsel had maliciously twisted the facts?

'That's all,' repeated Calaghan sharply, when Pawley remained in the witness-box. Calaghan was unconcerned about Pawley's reputation and as far as the game register was concerned, it mattered not how Pawley had obtained it. Pawley could be proved to be a psychopath and it would not affect the figures of game shot on the fourth of December one little jot.

Pawley finally left the box. Several witnesses were called whose evidence was more or less formal, then the Decker family solicitor went into the witness-box. He was a small, precise man with the habit of rubbing forefinger and thumb together whilst he spoke.

'Will you please tell the court in the simplest form the terms of the trust that was created by Fawcett John deCourcy Decker.'

'The trust was created in nineteen hundred and fifty four, after extensive consultations with counsel. Mr Decker, sole owner of the estate, by which I mean Hurstley Place and the several farms belonging to it, gave the estate to the trust absolutely, thereby divesting himself of any rights in it. At the same time, Mrs Lydia Decker gave up all and any rights she had, or might have, in this same estate.'

'What was the reason for doing this?'

'The desire to avoid the payment of death duties. Once the gift was five years old, by law no death duties would be payable on Mr Decker's death.'

'What were the terms of this trust?'

'The estate was to be held in trust until Fawcett Decker, the son, reached the age of thirty-five. On that day he was to elect whether to accept the estate, or not. If he refused it, it would go to his younger brother, Mr Julian Decker.'

'Was the trust effective?'

'It was. Mr Fawcett John deCourcy Decker lived for two days beyond the end of the five year period and so the estate was exempt from death duties. I might add that at that time there was not the present graded scale allowing lesser duty on a death in the third, fourth, or fifth year, so that full duties were avoided by those two days.'

'Do you know when Mr Fawcett Decker

would have attained the age of thirty-five?'

'On January the fourth of next year.'

'In other words, one month after his death?'

'Yes.'

'Did you know what decision Mr Fawcett Decker had reached in respect of accepting or rejecting his inheritance under the trust?'

'No, sir.'

'What is the effect of his death?'

'The estate is inherited by Mr Julian Decker.'

Welter cross-examined briefly. 'Were you aware that the deceased had long since decided to renounce his claim under the trust due to the sad fact that his expectation of life was at all times nil?'

'I had no knowledge of this.'

'You cannot deny that this is so, then, if I call witnesses to such effect?'

'Obviously not.'

'Was the object of the trust simply and solely to avoid death duties?'

'As I have already said, yes, that was the object. It was perfectly legal.'

'If Mr Fawcett Decker had inherited the estate and had then died soon afterwards, as was almost inevitable, would death duties have had to be paid?'

'They would.'

'Would he have known this?'

'I cannot say.'

'Surely it's reasonable to suppose he did?'

'I would think so.'

'Then it's very unlikely indeed that he would ever have accepted the estate?'

'I cannot say.'

'But knowing how the Decker family did everything in their power to keep the estate intact...'

'No, no, Mr Welter,' interrupted the judge, 'this is pure supposition. You know better than to try to introduce such evidence.'

Welter bowed, a trifle ironically, at the Bench. He addressed the witness again. 'There is, is there not, a rule under English law by which the perpetrator of a crime may not benefit from his crime?'

'There is.'

'If Mr Julian Decker killed his brother in order to inherit the estate, then this law would prevent his inheriting it?' Welter paused, to allow the jury to understand fully the meaning of his words. 'That surely makes nonsense of the alleged motive for this crime?'

The witness made no answer. Welter sat down.

Calaghan re-examined. 'If the accused had shot his brother and his crime had gone unpunished, would he then have been legally entitled to inherit the estate?'

'He would.'

'Thank you.'

The witness left the box. Welter watched him walk to one of the benches and sit down and wondered, morosely, whether it had been a bad mistake to try to make that last point.

Doherty was called. His evidence was only partially heard when the judge called a halt and adjourned the court for the day.

★ ★ ★ ★

Even his short period of imprisonment, or remand in custody as it was more politely called, had taught Julian that there were grades of criminals. Being on remand, he was not at night-time held in the main part of the prison but in one of the wings where there was little contact with other prisoners: even so, two men separately had told him the previous night what they thought of someone depraved enough to shoot his own crippled brother. It was all a question of status, he'd thought with bitter irony. If he'd shot a policeman, he would no doubt have been a hero. Just now, when a warder had brought him his dinner—he was not to return to prison from the cell under the courtroom until eight o'clock—the warder had slammed the tray down on the bunk and said that the grub was far too good for a bastard who shot his own brother. What sort of food was suitable for a train robber, a rapist, or a child murderer?

He stared at the half roast chicken, fried potatoes, peas, brown bread and butter, and the fruit salad and cream. To be tried for a crime when guilty of it was a frightening thing: but to be innocent and yet know a verdict of guilty must be brought in was a thousand times more frightening. In war, men were often tortured to give information. If they had information to give, eventually they could break down, give it, and so be released from the torture: but if they knew nothing, there could be no end to the torture.

He wanted to shout, to slam his fists

against the brick walls, to seek pain in order to relieve the fear in his mind, but he did nothing. Even as he longed to act, part of his mind assured him of the futility of such action.

How could they believe he had shot Fawcett? How could they have missed the one successful point that Welter had made? Fawcett would not have taken the estate because he might have died the next year and he would never have so jeopardised Hurstley Place. Hurstley Place was infinitely bigger than any Decker. Why couldn't the people in court understand that? The motive ascribed to the murder was so utterly ridiculous. Any Decker might kill to save Hurstley Place, but the killing of Fawcett was meaningless.

He lit a cigarette and noticed how his hands were trembling. It took so little to topple a man into the dust. An empty cartridge case, a game counter, one or two facts, one or two theories, and he was no longer Julian Decker of Hurstley Place, but was Decker the bastard who's shot his brother for the loot.

Barbara would be giving evidence tomorrow. How in God's name was he going to be able to bear seeing her in the witness-box? They weren't content with putting him on the cross, they had to make her suffer as well. How much was she suffering? It could be even more than he because she had the added burden of the guilt of freedom. That was a phrase he remembered having read a few years before. When there were two people close together of whom only one directly suffered, the other indirectly suffered because of the guilt of freedom: freedom, or innocence, became a terrible burden. Suppose he were imprisoned for life? What would she do? Would she always mourn? Of course not. Time would eventually come to her help. She would one day be able to forget that he was mouldering away in some prison.

The warder came in, saw he had not eaten, and told him roughly to get a move on as there was not much time left. He suddenly felt hungry. He ate.

Throughout the journey to the prison in the Black Maria, his mind focused on Barbara. He tried to recall every inch of her face, the way her mouth twisted just before she smiled, how she'd hold his hand. The memories brought on bitterness that increased until his mind became a cauldron of emotion. The warder, beyond the last cell-like compartment, stared hard at him as if believing he might be about to try to escape. He remembered when Barbara and he had walked slowly through the cherry orchard at blossom time. They had sworn they would plant a cherry orchard in the park so that they could always remember that day. It had been uninhibited sentimentalism and they had revelled in it. Now, the memory of those blossoms mocked him.

Inside the prison, the Black Maria stopped quite near the gates so that when he was let out of the back he was in time to see two warders swinging the double gates shut. They came together with a deep clang. He was inside and Barbara was outside and never the twain should meet. The warder who had been in the van shouted at him to get moving because he wasn't bloody well going to stay there all night.

He and Barbara were to have been married soon. A lot of the arrangements were already made. He remembered his mother had suggested a firm of caterers who did absolutely everything for the bride: she had said that they even sent telegrams of congratulations when too few could normally be expected. That was probably nonsense. His mother often got hold of the wrong end of the stick in things that didn't matter: things that did matter, however, found her sharper than the proverbial needle.

He remembered Barbara the last time they had allowed their passion a free run. She had not wanted to stop any more than he had, but somehow they had managed to because they both wanted to leave the final act of love making until after they were married. There was nothing prudish here—they merely knew how much more wonderful their marriage would be if they did this.

The warder took hold of his arm in a harsh grip and warned him not to make trouble.

'Trouble?' queried Julian, bewildered.

'I've told you to move three times and you've gone on standing there. You start anything, mate, and it'll be me what finishes it even if you are a bloody aristocrat.'

Did the oaf really think he'd been about to start trouble? He began to walk. They went up stone steps, along a passage, and climbed the circular stairs. All the time, his mind mocked him by reminding him how she had looked that last time when he had drawn away and stared down at her. Her eyes were closed, her mouth was slightly open, and she had appeared almost to be in pain because the fires of passion hadn't yet all been put out.

'Get in,' muttered the warder.

He went into the cell, sat down on the uncomfortable bunk, and rested his head on his hands. If he could make his memory commit suicide, he would: but he knew that nothing would kill it. Other images came. Himself and Barbara doing this or that.

The cell door opened and a trusty stepped inside. 'Want anything?'

Because he was on remand and might, in theory, be found innocent at his trial so that his imprisonment would be wrong, he was granted a number of 'privileges.' Right now, he could ask for a hot drink, something to eat, newspapers, or books.

'I said, d'you want anything, mate?'

He looked up at the trusty. Was this how he would look and behave after seven years of imprisonment: a human husk inside which most human attributes had withered? He cursed. He was innocent. To hell with how the trial had gone, to hell with his own counsel. He was innocent. There must be some way of proving it. 'Are there any law books in the library?'

The trusty stared with perplexity at him. 'Any what, mate?'

'Law books. Text books on criminal law.'

'Search me, mate.'

'If there are any, I want 'em.'

'I don't rightly know...'

Julian took a packet of cigarettes from his pocket. Even his short stay in prison had been long enough to teach him the purchasing power of a packet of cigarettes, full size and so many times fatter than the cigarettes the convicts rolled themselves.

The trusty took the cigarettes and then hurriedly left, pulling the heavy steel door shut after himself.

Julian rubbed his forehead with the back of his hand. Law books? What in the name of hell did he think he was going to do with them? Hadn't he one of the top criminal lawyers battling for him, so of what use could a law book conceivably be?

His mind recalled Barbara once more. He groaned. If only to God a man's mind could be imprisoned at the same time as was his body.

CHAPTER 16

For most of the following morning Doherty was in the witness-box. Because he gave his evidence very fairly, stressing no point beyond another, Welter found himself in a quandary when it came to cross-examination. He turned and spoke to his junior. 'Well, Felix?'

'You're the boss, not me,' replied Richie unhelpfully.

'Stop being so bloody craven, man. Do I tackle him on accident or don't I?'

'Can't you stall a bit longer?'

'No.'

The judge interrupted them. 'Mr Welter, I expect counsel to have completed their consultations before they come into my courtroom.'

'I'm sorry, my lord,' said Welter, turning round as he spoke. You old bastard, he thought: you know damned well this is the point of no return and I've got to make the decision. Welter looked at the back of the head of his instructing solicitor, who sat in front and below him. Cortelan had some time ago made the classic statement that on the one hand it would pay to introduce the defence of accident, but that on the other hand it would not.

Welter hooked his thumbs in the pockets of his waistcoat. For a few seconds he stared down at the folds in his gown, then he looked at the witness. 'Inspector, had you heard of the Decker family before this regrettable death?'

'Yes, sir.'

'What did you know about them?'

'That they owned a large estate.'

'Had you ever seen the house?'

'No, sir.'

'Or the grounds?'

'I've been past them, but I never knew which land belonged to the estate.'

'Would it be true to say that you were well aware that the Deckers were an old family and that they were, if one is still allowed to use such a phrase, of the landed gentry?'

'Yes, sir.'

'Were you aware before Mr Fawcett Decker's death that the estate belonged to a trust?'

'I was.'

'And were you aware of the terms of the trust?'

'I was.'

'You well knew that the whole estate was in trust for the elder son, Fawcett Decker, when he reached the age of thirty-five? That on his thirty-fifth birthday he must elect whether, or not, to accept the estate and that if he decided against it the estate would pass to the younger son, Julian Decker?'

'Yes, I did know that.'

'Then you were aware of a possible motive for the murder of the deceased some time before he died?'

'I wouldn't put it like that, sir.'

'But I would, Inspector. This means that when Fawcett Decker died you not only knew there could be a motive, but because you knew this you naturally thought of the death as a murder?'

'No, sir.'

'Then it is not true to say that you treated the death as a murder from the very beginning?'

'I took such steps as I deemed necessary, sir, and then awaited various reports, including those from the pathologist and the gun expert.'

'Yet surely we have earlier this morning heard you testify that on your arrival in the woods and after a brief inspection of the body you demanded two cartridges from each of the guns present?'

'I did, yes.'

'And you called in a photographer and had your men search the woods long before you ever received the reports from either the pathologist or the gun expert?'

'I was taking such steps as I deemed necessary, sir.'

'Inspector, I put it to you that quite clearly you treated this as a case of murder from the very beginning?'

'I took the steps I deemed necessary, sir,' repeated Doherty.

On the Bench, the judge wondered what line he would have taken had he been in Welter's shoes? Would he from the beginning have gone for a plea of accident and risked the effects of the introduction of the evidence of the other two deaths and of the motive behind them that so plainly was connected with the motive in this case? And what was Welter going to do now?

'I put it to you that your judgement was reached before you knew the facts on which to reach a judgment?' said Welter.

'That is not so, sir.'

Welter picked up his note-book and read through some notes. He put the note-book down and resumed his cross-examination.

★ ★ ★ ★

Brendon went into the witness-box at 2.30 in the afternoon. He had a confused character. For years he had acted as a beater on the Hurstley shoot and for years he had, during lunch and whilst drinking the free beer, condemned shooting as the sport of the degenerate and diseased aristocracy. He claimed to hate the Deckers and to despise all they represented, yet he never missed an opportunity to speak to any of the family. He called himself a communist, yet believed in royalty and never ceased recalling the time when royalty had come to Hurstley Place and had a word or two with him.

Calaghan, after putting the preliminary questions, wiped his forehead with his handkerchief. Avonley courtroom was one of the very few on the circuit that was kept warm and the world being a perverse one, it was kept too warm. 'Mr Brendon, were you out beating on Saturday, December the fourth?'

'I was.' Brendon had a squeaky voice. Behind his back he was called Blether-and Squeak.

'Will you tell the court whereabouts you were at King's Beat?'

'I was a stop at the old yew.'

'We shall have to take this a little slowly for the jury's sake. A stop is what?'

'He's the bloke what stays in one place to keep the birds from breaking out before the beaters come through.'

'Then he's ahead of the beaters?'

'Up near the flushing point, as often as not.'

'Have a look at the plan the usher will now hand you, please, and tell us exactly where the old yew is.'

Brendon was handed a photostat copy of the map of King's Beat. 'D'you see the ride that comes down and meets the ride what goes to the field? That's it. Where the wood comes out and meets the first ride, that's where we call the old yew because of a tree they say is as old as the hills.'

The judge spoke to the jury. 'Have you all found the place on your copies of the map?'

Some of the jury nodded.

'From where you were,' continued Calaghan, 'could you see any of the guns when they were at the stands?'

'You can't see nothing of them because of all the trees and undergrowth.'

'Could you see the ride that goes down and round the point of the woods: around the flushing point, I believe?'

'I could see down it until it went round the corner.'

'Will you tell us, in your own words, if you saw anyone on that ride after the guns had gone to their stands?'

'I was stop, like I said. I kept my stick tapping because if you don't the birds come out at that corner in busloads. I saw the guns go down the ride and some went to their stands and some went round and out of sight. After a bit, some high birds come over and one or two were shot. Mr Wade was at number seven. Missed a beauty, he did. Then Mr Fawcett comes down the ride, rushing his chair along like it was a racing car. I asked him what luck and he said he'd had a few back across the valley and a very good right and left. He carried on down the ride. Next thing, Miss Harmsworth comes down the ride from the field. She'd got her dog with her. I said good morning and she has a bit of a chat and says the scent's not very good. Then she goes down the ride.'

'Did you watch her?'

'Not all at once because I saw a lot of birds wanting to break past me so I taps like mad and they turned.'

'When did you look down the ride?'

'D'you mean how long after I first saw her?'

'If you can remember sufficiently accurately, but it's more important to say whom you saw on the ride the next time you looked down it.'

'There was Miss Harmsworth and Mr Julian and they was talking.'

'Whereabouts were they?'

'Just where the ride turned out of sight of me.'

'Would you say this would, on the map, be about opposite the tip of the flushing point?'

'Please don't lead,' objected Welter loudly.

Calaghan turned. 'Would you like me to call witnesses to prove that from the position where Mr Brendon was standing his line of view came to an end almost exactly opposite the tip of the flushing point?'

'You ought to have proved that before now.'

Calaghan addressed the witness again. 'Is that about the limit of view?'

'That's right.'

'And as we have already heard from another witness...' here Calaghan turned and looked at Welter, who ignored the gesture, '...this point is approximately midway between stands four and five. You saw Miss Harmsworth talking to Mr Julian Decker at this point after Mr Fawcett Decker had gone along the ride?'

'That's it.'

'One last question. Was Mr Julian Decker carrying his gun?'

There was a sudden silence: the strange, strained kind of silent that only occurs in a murder trial.

'He was,' said Brendon.

Welter cross-examined. 'Do *you* know for a fact that the point at which your view was shut off was a point mid-way between numbers four and five guns?'

'I've never checked, like, but...'

'How far away from you was Miss Harmsworth when she talked to this person on the ride?'

'It's difficult to say.'

'Will you accept my figure of about three hundred yards?'

'If you say so.'

'At three hundred yards, Mr Brendon, how can you be so very certain it was Mr Julian Decker you saw?'

'There weren't no mistake.'

'At three hundred yards, a man's features are not exactly clear-cut, are they?' Even as he continued the cross-examination, Welter knew that he could never gain the point he was trying to make.

* * * *

Barbara took the oath. She had looked once at Julian and smiled, then she carefully stared away from him. She gripped the edge of the witness-box with her gloved fingers as she answered the first few questions in a voice devoid of any inflexion.

'Miss Harmsworth,' said Calaghan, 'will you please tell us about your movements at King's Beat.'

'I came in from the field and walked down the ride. When I reached the turn of the ride I went left into the Larch Plantation which is where the high birds fall and most of the runners come.'

'Did you speak to anyone?'

'I said hallo to Mr Brendon who was by the old yew.'

'Anyone else?'

'No.'

'Miss Harmsworth, don't forget you are on oath.'

'I'm perfectly well aware of that,' she said loudly.

'Then you must realise that to lie is a very serious offence.'

'I am not lying.'

The judge spoke. 'Miss Harmsworth, we have heard that you are engaged to be married to the accused. It is, therefore, natural that you should want to assist your fiancé in every possible way, but this is a court of law and in a court of law you owe an absolute duty to the truth.'

'I swear I'm not lying.'

After a quick look at the judge, who nodded, Calaghan said: 'Before you say anything more, Miss Harmsworth, I think you should know that the last witness was Mr Brendon. He has testified that he spoke to you and that a short while later he saw you on the ride, at the point opposite mid-way between number four and number five stands, talking to the accused.'

She began to shiver and those close enough could see her strain at the side of the box with her hands to control herself. She began to cry and she turned and looked at Julian. All the agony in her mind was apparent in her face.

Julian, for one second of exploding hatred, was about to fight his way to her. The warder sensed this and gripped his right arm. Slowly, he relaxed.

★ ★ ★ ★

Lydia Decker was called by the defence just before the end of the second day. For once, she had dressed with care.

'Were you aware of the terms of the trust set up by your husband?' asked Welter.

'I was.' Some of the onlookers, seeing how upright she stood and how firm her expression, and hearing how strong and level was her voice, judged her to be an arrogant old woman: they failed completely to realise she was an old woman who was showing all the pluck in the world.

'You knew that your elder son, on reaching the age of thirty-five, would have to elect whether or not to accept the estate?'

'He wasn't going to.'

'He wasn't going to what, Mrs Decker?'

'He was not going to accept the estate. There was never any possibility that he would. He was not expected to live nearly as long as he did and he knew that as well as we did. His illness could have killed him at any time. On the day of my husband's funeral, we discussed the matter and Fawcett told me that he would never inherit the estate because of the danger of doing so.'

There was no objection to this hearsay.

'Fawcett loved Hurstley Place,' continued Lydia Decker, and just once there was a break in her voice. 'He knew the history of the family and the house as well as I do. He would have done anything to preserve the estate and nothing would have induced him to accept it when he became thirty-five. Only a few days before his death, he told Julian and me that on his birthday he would renounce his claim so that the estate could immediately vest in Julian. In that way, when Julian married and had a son there would be another generation of Deckers for Hurstley Place.'

'Thank you, Mrs Decker.'

Calaghan hesitated and then decided not to cross-examine. The court was adjourned for the day.

★ ★ ★ ★

That night, Julian knew even greater mental agony than ever before. He had seen his fiancé fight for him, lose the fight, and leave the box in a state of collapse: he had seen his mother fight for him with every ounce of her indomitable courage and yet waste all her efforts. He was bound to be found guilty on the evidence given, bound to be condemned to imprisonment for life, bound to be the last male Decker to live at Hurstley Place.

He lit a cigarette. On the far end of the bunk were the three law books that had been brought to him the previous night by the trusty. Each book was thumbed dirty, sometimes to the point of illegibility. Tens of men, perhaps hundreds, had read those books with the same desperation that he had, trying to find an escape from the remorseless grip of the law. Yet how many of them would have been as he was, innocent of the crime for which he was going to be found guilty?

He dropped the cigarette on to the floor and ground it out with his shoe, in deliberate and juvenile contradiction of the rule that prisoners would at all times keep their cells clean and tidy. Justice had become a word of mockery. Innocence was a farce. God Almighty, how was a man to remain sane when he fought injustice but knew he must lose no matter how hard he fought?

He went to the end of the bunk and picked up the thickest of the law books. It was stuffed full of learning. It represented centuries of English law, renowned for its fairness. Surely somewhere in this tome he would discover how an innocent man was allowed to prove his innocence?

CHAPTER 17

The third day of the trial opened. The judge came on to the dais escorted by his clerk, the lawyers bowed, the judge briefly returned their bows and sat down, and everyone else sat down. The sounds of shuffling feet, coughing, and sneezing, gradually died away.

Welter stood up and prepared to resume the defence, but he was suddenly interrupted.

'I want to defend myself,' called out Julian.

Surprise was general and the noise of talking grew. Welter stared at Julian with angry amazement as the judge spoke and said that this was an exceedingly unwise course of action to take and that no accused could better defend himself than he could be defended by counsel. The judge suggested in strong terms that Julian reconsider his decision. Julian repeated his demand. The judge, with icy disapproval, said that he could not prevent such a thing. He asked Welter to be kind enough to remain in court.

'Do you wish to give evidence?' asked the judge. 'You may either make an unsworn statement from the dock, on which you will not be cross-examined, or you may go into the witness-box, take the oath, and give your evidence, whereupon you will be liable to be cross-examined. It is my duty to point out to you that a jury will rightly place more weight on evidence given on oath than on an unsworn statement.'

'I'll go into the witness-box.'

'Mr Decker, I should feel in dereliction of my duty if I did not once more try to persuade you to revoke your decision to defend yourself.'

'I know what I'm doing.'

'Very well,' snapped the judge.

The warder unbolted the door at the side of the dock and Julian went down the three wooden steps and walked along the gangway between the witness's benches and counsel's benches. He felt, almost as a physical force, the impact of concentrated gaze of all those present. He entered the witness-box and took the oath, handing both the card and the New Testament back to the usher when he had finished speaking.

Just for a second, his nerve almost failed him. This was a gamble that was almost suicidal. If he failed... Yet Hurstley Place was at stake. It was a gamble he had to take. He began to give his evidence.

'On Saturday, the guns met in front of the house just before nine-thirty, as usual. We moved off in two Land-Rovers to the duck ponds for the drive there and then we went to The Springs and Park Wood. After Park Wood we drove back to the road and round to Hammotts Lane. We crossed the fifteen acre field and parked the cars by the entrance into the woods of King's Beat.

'I helped Fawcett unload his wheel-chair, using the special ramps. He was number one gun and so went into the woods and up to the right along the ride, in order to come down with the beaters and take the birds breaking to the left. More than once in the past I'd tried to persuade him not to take number one gun because it meant he had to cover so much ground in his wheel-chair, but he always got angry with me for suggesting this. He said that the day he couldn't be a normal gun, he'd give up shooting.

'The rest of us went down the ride to our stands. On the way I had a few words with my cousin, Mr Henry Decker, suggesting he should take number four's birds if he got the chance as number four would never hit them.

'I went to my stand at number five. A couple of fast, swerving pigeons came over and I got one of them. A high pheasant came over and I killed it. A little later on, two pheasants came between me and number six and although they were his birds I shot them.

'Just after this there was a movement in the undergrowth to my right and when I looked down I saw a flash of brown which I was certain was a fox, but I couldn't fire because I hadn't had the chance finally to identify it and it was pretty well in line with the other guns. I waited and a few seconds later a large dog fox came in view round one of the back pollard willow trees. As I raised my gun, it saw me and tried to run back into cover, but I put one barrel into it and knocked it over. Although I thought I'd killed it, when I went to look I obviously hadn't as there was no sign of it. I thought I heard a movement between me and the ride, so I pushed my way through. The birds were beginning to come over now, but I naturally wanted to put the fox out of its agony. I reached the ride without having found anything.

Miss Harmsworth came down the ride and asked me why I wasn't at the stand. I told her what had happened and asked her to keep a lookout for the fox in the Larch Plantation when she was in there picking-up. We parted and I went back to my stand. At the end of the beat I picked up the birds I could find and then returned to the ride to see Miss Harmsworth and tell her whereabouts the others were. Whilst I was there my headkeeper, Adams, came running up to say he had just found my brother dead.

'I went along the ride to the wheel-chair. It was... It was obvious my brother was dead and so I gave orders for the police to be called.

'I do not know who shot Fawcett. I did not see him again alive after he left to go up the ride at the beginning of the beat. Fawcett and I were not only brothers, we were also friends, and nothing on God's earth would have caused me to shoot him.

'It had long ago been agreed that I should inherit the estate because it seemed obvious I would live very much longer than he. This was Fawcett's decision, made because the only thing any of us worried about was Hurstley Place and that it should continue to belong to the Decker family. When I inherited the estate after Fawcett's thirty-fifth birthday, I was clearly going to make certain that Fawcett had whatever financial allowance he needed or wanted.'

After Julian finished speaking, there was a pause. The shorthand writer massaged his right forefinger, the clerk of the court shuffled some of his papers, two of the jurymen whispered together, and the judge for some time continued to write in his note-book.

Calaghan waited until the judge had finished writing and then stood up. 'You claim that an amicable agreement had been reached between you and your brother as to the disposition of the estate after he reached his thirty-fifth birthday, which would have been on January the fourth?'

'Yes.' The sense of panic within Julian's mind had grown until he had difficulty in overcoming it. Had he been a bloody fool to sack his counsel? Yet what other chance had there been?'

'What proof have you of this?'

'The family always knew what was going to happen.'

'I asked for proof. Were any documents drawn up and signed?'

'No.'

'Why not?'

'Because this was purely a family affair.'

'No matter how much of a family affair, surely one would expect a decision so eventful to be documented?'

'There was no need.'

'That is all you can answer?'

'It's the truth.'

'Very well. Let's examine another question. Since your brother had so far outlived the prognosis of all doctors, was there any real and valid reason to suppose he might not continue to live to reach a ripe old age?'

'He was liable to die at any minute.'

'But was he?'

'Yes.'

'How much is the estate worth?'

'I don't know.'

'But you must be able to make a very accurate guess. Is land worth about two hundred pounds an acre in your area?'

'Perhaps.'

'Then all the land, together with the buildings and farmhouses, must be worth about half a million pounds. Half a million pounds is a very great sum of money, isn't it?'

'Obviously.'

'But you invite the jury to believe that so large a fortune was so casually to be given up by your brother?'

'I've told you that his only concern was with the continuation of Hurstley Place.'

'Do you see any significance in the fact that his death took place only one month before he was due to make his election?'

'No.'

'I suggest that on the contrary there is a very great deal of significance in this fact. I suggest that your brother had no intention of renouncing his claim to an estate worth over half a million pounds and...'

'He was never going to accept it.'

'...And that you knew you had to murder him very soon or it would be too late.'

'No. I didn't kill him. Nothing on God's earth would have made me kill him.'

'Tell me, what means have you?'

'Means?'

'What fortune do you possess in your own right?'

'I have a little money.'

'How little?'

'About five thousand pounds.'

'Anything else?'

'No.'

'Then if you did not inherit the estate you could find yourself in a very difficult financial position?'

'Not exactly. I...'

'Suppose the estate had gone to your brother—how would you have earned a living?'

'That didn't arise. My job was running the estate.'

'Are you, then, admitting that you had no plans at all on how to earn a living if your brother decided to accept the inheritance?'

'He wasn't going to.'

'Or had you decided he wasn't to be allowed to?'

'I'm telling the truth.'

Calaghan shrugged his shoulders. 'Let's move on to the events that took place on the fourth of December. Did you leave the house for any reason before nine-thirty?'

'I went down before breakfast to Home

Farm and had a word with the farm manager.'

'Did you return to the house from there?'

'Yes.'

'You didn't go into any of the woods?'

'No.'

'At nine-thirty you set out with the other guns on the day's shooting. You went first to the duck ponds, then to The Springs and Park Wood. Are either of these two woods near King's Beat?'

'They're at least half a mile away.'

'So at no time were you anywhere near King's Beat before you went there to shoot?'

'No.'

'You drove up to the entrance to the woods and helped your brother to disembark. He went one way and you went the other, in company with the rest of the guns. You had a quick word with your cousin, Mr Henry Decker, and afterwards went on to number five stand. Up to the moment you went to your stand you had not fired your gun since leaving the Land-Rover. Is all that true?'

'Yes.'

'You shot a pigeon and three pheasants

after which you fired at a fox. You're certain you hit the fox. Were all those shots taken at the stand?'

'Yes.'

'You went back to the ride, searching for the wounded fox and there you met Miss Harmsworth. Did you fire your gun whilst you were on this ride?'

'No.'

'Then in view of all this evidence will you tell the court how a cartridge case, fired by your gun that morning, was found near the body of Fawcett Decker?'

'I never fired a cartridge there.'

'But the cartridge case *was* found and it *was* fired in your gun.' Calaghan picked up a sheet of paper and read it. 'Do you dispute the fact that you shot fifty-one pheasants on the shoot of November the twentieth?'

'No.'

'At the end of a shooting day, after you have entered your bag in the game-book, do you return your counter to zero? Or do you do this at the beginning of the next day's shooting?'

'When I've entered the figures in the game-book.'

'So on December the fourth your game

counter would have been recording zero?'

'It should have been, but I don't know for certain. I couldn't find the counter. I searched the gun-room for it.'

'When that counter was found in the turn-up of your brother's trousers, it recorded thirty-six. Do you accept the fact that up to the beginning of King's Beat no one else had shot more than twenty pheasants?'

'I can't prove otherwise.'

'And you had shot thirty-three?'

'Yes. But I lost the counter and didn't have it.'

'The prosecution has shown that your brother came along the ride in his wheelchair before Miss Harmsworth walked along it and that therefore he passed along it very early in the beat—after only a few birds had gone over the guns. You shot three pheasants at this early stage. When the counter was found it recorded thirty-six, which we know to be the number of birds you had shot up to the time you returned to the ride?'

'I lost the counter. I lost it. Can't you understand?'

'Quite so, you did lose it. But not at the beginning of the day, was it? It was after you'd shot your brother and had gone up to the body to make certain he was dead. It fell unseen out of your pocket and into the turn-up of your brother's trousers. It is a damning piece of evidence because it is unquestionably yours, it is set at the number of birds you had unquestionably shot, and the figure of thirty-six unquestionably cannot refer to any of the other guns.'

'I didn't kill Fawcett.'

'You were desperate because, after years of managing the estate and looking on it as yours, you were suddenly forced to realise it was never going to be yours. Your brother had decided to accept his inheritance. To you, there was only one course of action left. To murder your brother so that he couldn't inherit the estate. You were going to make the murder look like an accident. At King's Beat he was number one gun, which meant that after the other guns had taken up position he would come down the ride...'

'I didn't murder him,' shouted Julian. 'I couldn't have murdered my brother. You're trying me because you know I was convicted of manslaughter by shooting several years ago. That makes you think...'

'Be quiet,' interrupted the judge. He put down his pencil and addressed prosecuting counsel. 'Mr Calaghan?'

Calaghan answered. 'I fear I cannot help your lordship.'

The judge looked for several seconds at Julian before he spoke to him. His voice was harsh. 'The law says that when the accidental disclosure of a previous conviction takes place in the trial of an undefended prisoner it is the duty of the judge to tell the prisoner that he has the right to apply that the jury be discharged and the trial be started afresh. If you wish to make such an application, you must do so now.'

'I want a new trial,' replied Julian hoarsely.

CHAPTER 18

Julian paced his cell—a cell he now knew intimately. He thought about all that had happened. He had gained himself a respite and his trial would have to be held again, but what had he accomplished in actual fact? Anything? The facts wouldn't alter for the second trial. The evidence would still point to him as the murderer. Yet he had stopped the law steam-rollering over him, he had delayed the law's verdict, and even that much was something of a miracle.

Now he had to see Barbara and gain her help. For the first time he suddenly wondered how far she would help him? He was going to ask her to break the law in more than one way: would she? Suppose that by now she secretly believed he had killed Fawcett, would she help him? Would she help a murderer just because she had been engaged to him? Could she still love a man she believed to have committed fratricide? If a woman loved a man as she had loved him, how much was her love affected by something he did that did not directly affect her? Angrily, he shook his head as if to deny words spoken aloud. Imprisonment was warping his mind. Barbara believed him utterly and suffered no doubts. She was possessed of that rare kind of loyalty which meant she would do anything in her power to help him. Another question filled his mind. Was he justified in demanding she take such a risk? But there was only one answer to this if he were ever to have the chance to prove his innocence. If...

He paced the floor of the cell. He had to be one jump ahead of the prosecution. Which way would they go, knowing they had to be one jump ahead of him? Who would leapfrog over whom? They believed they were fighting for justice, he knew he was fighting for justice and Hurstley Place. Who was better armed? 'Thrice is he armed that hath his quarrel just.'

★ ★ ★ ★

Detective Superintendent Quincy went into Avonley Police Station and to the D.I's room. He gave a perfunctory knock on the door, entered, kicked the door shut, and began to strip off his wet raincoat.

'It's raining buckets, Sam. It's raining enough to float off the whole bloody countryside into the sea.'

Doherty, sitting at his desk, turned round and looked through the window. The glass was so wet that everything beyond it appeared distorted and the chimney stack seemed to be twisting in all directions. 'It is raining.'

'Why so surprised? Been asleep for the past two hours?'

'I've been trying to catch up on the paper-work, sir. H.Q often seems to think we haven't anything else to do.'

'It's only the paper-work that proves half the divisional D.Is aren't on holiday. The crime figures suggest they are.'

Doherty smiled.

Quincy hung his dripping raincoat on the battered mahogany stand. He walked over to the desk and sat down on the edge. 'The clear-up rate for the county stinks.'

'Maybe that's because there's too much paper-work to cope with.'

Quincy swore.

Doherty took a packet of cigarettes from his pocket and offered it. Quincy accepted a cigarette and a light. 'The bastard,' he said.

'Which one in particular?'

'Which one d'you think has got under my skin and found all the tender parts? Decker.'

Doherety spoke reflectively. 'He's certainly managed to throw a spanner in the works.'

'Spanner? It was a ruddy big girder. Why did they let him get away with it? Goddamn it, man, the prosecution and the judge weren't given any list of previous convictions so they must have known Decker was pulling a fast one.'

'They didn't have any option, did they? The law's quite mandatory—since no one's ever envisaged a prisoner admitting to false previous convictions. In the circumstances, the judge had to give Decker the opportunity to call for a new trial: after all, it could just have been true in that Decker might have once been convicted under a false name.'

'The routine fingerprint check would have cleared that up.'

'That's been known to go wrong in the past. Anyway, the judge just didn't have any option in the matter. And did that make him spit tacks!'

'It makes me spit bloody great long nails. What a waste of public money?'

'I doubt Decker sees the thing quite in that light.'

'Decker's a... Now listen to me, Sam, it's not going to happen again and that's an order. Have you sent his fingerprints out again and demanded definite, absolute, and irrefutable proof that Mr Julian Decker has never before been convicted of anything stronger than parking without lights?'

'Yes, sir.'

Quincy stared at the D.I for a while. 'Hell,' he said suddenly, 'this second trial means you, Pawley, and God knows how many other of my detectives will be tied up in court again. How's any of the work going to get done?'

'I suppose in the usual way. Some of us will work a pile of overtime for which we won't get paid.'

'Now look, Sam, if you're after a nine to five job, paid holidays, and fringe benefits by the dozen, you'd better change to the civil service.'

'I've often thought about it. I'm too old now, though.'

'Why the devil don't you return to Ireland and buy yourself a plot in the local churchyard?'

They became silent and could hear the rain as it beat on the window-panes.

'They'll nail him this next time,' said Quincy loudly.

'I suppose so.'

'It's your case, man. You shouldn't damn' well suppose: you should know.'

'I've never been completely happy with the facts.'

'One look at your face is enough to tell

anyone you're never happy about anything,' retorted Quincy sourly. 'You know your trouble, don't you? You're pig-headed. There's enough evidence in this case to hang the man twice over, if those stupid bastards in parliament hadn't abolished hanging. Just look at it. He stands to make half a million, he's seen close to the murder spot with his gun, the job was done with the load from a sixteen bore and he's the only one with a sixteen bore apart from the dead man, a sixteen bore cartridge case fired that day and in his gun is found near the body, and his game counter is in the dead man's turn-up, set at the right figure. What more d'you want? A written confession in triplicate? And what about all the evidence that's never ever been touched on in court? What about the other two murders?'

'I'll give you those first two.'

'That's too bloody generous of you.'

Doherty spoke slowly. 'A Decker would kill to save the estate: he'd go so far as see it to be his duty. But I just can't get used to the idea of a Decker killing a Decker.'

'There's half a million quid at stake, Sam. Most people would murder every living relative for just half of that.'

'The money wouldn't count in this case. I've always seen the money as something of a motive tailored to suit the facts.'

'Then was it coincidence that Fawcett Decker was killed within one month of having to elect whether or not to take the estate? Of course it wasn't, Sam, and you know it wasn't. You're too good a detective to be so stupid. It's in your bones like it's in mine that this period of a month is at the core of the case: this month meant that the murder had to be committed when it was.'

'I still don't see a Decker shooting his brother. I said it before and I say it again.'

'I reckon that woman, Mrs Decker, bewitched you. After being with her for five minutes you won't hear a word against the whole ruddy family. If they'd butchered every inhabitant in the local village, you'd just sit there and find a string of excuses for them.'

'The last murder is psychologically wrong.'

'Stuff psychology. What about the facts?'

'I know, I know. They're not easy to walk round.'

'You shouldn't even be trying to walk round 'em.'

'I suppose you're right again, sir.'

'Then just leave the psychology to people stupid enough to be able to spell it.' Quincy stared out of the window. 'It's raining harder than ever. I tell you, this time tomorrow we'll all find ourselves washed into the bloody sea.'

★ ★ ★ ★

Julian, in his cell, looked at his watch. In two minutes he should be seeing Barbara. For the umpteenth time he told himself that when he did see her he must suppress all the emotions which would so desperately be wanting to break free.

He checked on his watch again: one minute to go. Would she be dressed smartly, to cheer him up, or would that seem to her too much like celebrating a funeral?

It was time now, but no one came to the cell for him. Had something gone wrong? Perhaps she'd decided at the last minute that she couldn't face the visit. It needed a special kind of a courage willingly to see one's fiancé in prison. Or perhaps she had suddenly been taken ill or met with an accident? He remembered when she had once been forty minutes late because of a puncture in the open countryside and how he had imagined during the last thirty minutes that she had suffered every conceivable accident or outrage.

He lit a cigarette. If she hadn't come by the time he had finished the cigarette, he'd know that something... He heard the sounds of a key being inserted in the lock and turned. The bolts were withdrawn and the door was opened.

'Visiting,' said the warder. 'Follow me.'

Julian followed the other along the corridor. This warder seemed to think there was a tax on words: in two days he had hardly spoken a sentence of more than four words.

They went down circular stairs, along the passage way at the bottom, and came to a halt in front of a steel door. The warder knocked on the door, a small peep-hole was opened up, and an eye surveyed them. The eye disappeared, the peep-hole was closed, and the door was opened.

Like some piece of important diplomatic baggage, Julian was officially handed from one warder's charge to the other's. He found himself wildly wondering why he wasn't labelled with his destination. Then, he was shown into the visiting room and he saw Barbara.

She was wearing the suit that she had worn when he proposed to her and she, without the slightest hesitation, had accepted his proposal.

Between them was a table that ran the length of the room. Above the table was a thick glass partition and below it a solid partition. There were six pairs of chairs and between each pair, in the glass partition, was a speaking place.

They stared at each other.

'Sit down,' ordered the warder.

He sat down. Here, he was not even allowed the freedom to decide whether to sit or stand.

'How is it, darling?' she asked.

'Not as bad as it might have been.'

'Your mother sends her love.'

'How's she taking things?'

'Quite well, really. She keeps saying she's feeling very old, but she's doing twice as much cleaning and polishing as ever.'

She was probably feeling very old and very defeated, he thought. Defeat would be infinitely the more bitter of the two.

'What about you?'

'I'm fine, darling.'

She was exercising the traditional English approach by which, in the middle of catastrophe, all was made to appear normal.

'Barbara,' he said and then checked his words.

'Well?'

'Will you...do something for me?'

'Why do you have to ask?'

'It could mean trouble.'

'Just tell me what you want.'

He looked sideways, at the warder. The man, too far away to hear easily, was studying Barbara with lascivious interest. 'Go up to London,' he said, 'and see a solicitor. It doesn't matter who just so long as he's no idea who you are. Then...' Julian went on speaking, in as low a voice as was possible.

★ ★ ★ ★

The second trial of Julian Decker was held in the same courtroom and before the same judge. He was represented by the same counsel and Calaghan was again prosecuting. Only the members of the jury were different.

Before the opening speech for the prosecution, the judge addressed the jury. 'You will all have read in the papers, or seen on television, or listened on the wireless, to descriptions or comments on a previous trial. I now direct you that on no account are you to take note of anything you have previously heard, seen, or read. Your duty is to try the accused solely on the evidence you hear in this court.' The judge looked at Calaghan. 'Very well.'

'My lord and members of the jury, this is a trial for murder. Murder is defined as the taking of life with malice aforethought, either express or implied, by a person sound in mind.

In the present case, I suggest that there can be no doubt...'

★ ★ ★ ★

The trial proceeded slightly more quickly than had the first one and Lydia Decker completed giving her evidence just before four o'clock on the second day. When she left the witness-box, she walked to one of the benches with the upright carriage of someone who would never bend before fate. But she was looking very old; her face was heavily lined and the flesh about her cheeks seemed to have shrunk.

Counsel looked pointedly at the clock. 'Well,' snapped the judge, 'who's your next witness?'

Welter sighed. With a dinner-party at home that evening, he had hoped to catch an early train back to London. 'I call the accused, Mr Julian Decker.'

Julian was escorted to the witness-box by the warder. The usher came forward and Julian took the oath.

After the preliminary questions, Welter leaned back against the bench behind him. 'Mr Decker, I want you now to tell the jury in your own words what kind of relationship existed between yourself and the deceased, your brother, Fawcett Decker?'

Julian made no answer.

Welter's voice rose slightly. 'Will you please tell the court what was the relationship between your brother and yourself?'

'I want to conduct my defence,' said Julian.

There was a sudden clamour of conversation that swelled in volume until it became almost a roar. The usher and the policeman on duty by the main doors called repeatedly for silence. After a while, the noise died down.

The judge spoke to counsel. 'Mr Welter, were you aware that this was going to happen?'

'Indeed not, my lord. Had I had the slightest idea, I would have...' He stopped before he said something that might compromise his client.

The judge leaned back in his red-leather, gold-crested chair. On the wall behind him, the carved wooden scales of justice remained in eternal equilibrium. 'I have no intention of allowing the law or this court to be mocked,' he said flatly. 'The jury will retire.'

For a while, the courtroom was noisy to the sounds of shuffling feet, then the door was closed behind the jury. The judge spoke to the Press benches. 'I would ask you not to publish any part of what follows.' He turned to the witness-box. 'I propose to make myself quite clear. At a previous trial, a similar demand by you to conduct your own trial led to a position in which I was forced by the rules of procedure governing this court to give you the chance to demand a fresh trial. It had not escaped the court's attention that a malicious attempt to produce a similar abandonment of this second trial might be made. I therefore warn you, in the strongest possible terms, that no attempt of this nature can succeed. I suggest that in your own interests you withdraw your decision to defend yourself and that you allow this trial to continue in its present form.'

'Am I not now allowed to defend myself?'

The judge's voice became harsher. 'I cannot forbid you to do so.'

'Then I'll defend myself.'

The judge stared at Julian for some time, then leaned forward and picked up one of the text books. He read through two pages before putting down the book, open, on his desk. 'Mr Welter, do you imagine it will be of the slightest use your having a talk with the accused? As much as my inclination might be to allow him to suffer the fruits of his own folly, I feel obliged to do everything possible to avoid this.'

'I could speak to him, my lord.'

'Will you do so, please. If you require a short adjournment, the court will grant one and even, if necessary, will adjourn until to-morrow.'

Welter walked along the row of benches. Calaghan, in the row behind as he was not a silk, spoke as Welter came level. 'You picked a ripe one!'

'Over-ripe, and if I don't soon get a train home I'll be late for my own dinner-party.' He went into the gangway and across to the witness-box. 'Mr Decker, stop being a fool.'

'Am I?'

'Yes.'

'How else can I get anywhere? What odds will you offer me on a verdict of not guilty?'

'I've been doing my best,' said Welter stiffly.

'But your best can't possibly be good enough.'

Welter turned and faced the Bench. 'My lord, it's obvious that there's no chance I shall be able to persuade the accused to change his mind.'

'Would it not be best to take a short adjournment, Mr Welter, so that you may discuss the matter far more fully than you have done?'

'The accused has, my lord, even in

so short a time made it perfectly clear that there is nothing to be gained by an adjournment.'

The judge tapped his fingers on the desk. He looked at the clock on the wall, at Calaghan, and then back at Welter. 'Mr Welter, this is an intolerable situation. The court owes a duty to a prisoner to see that he does not place himself in greater peril than he is already in, but no court can fulfil such obligation in face of the prisoner's hostility. Nevertheless, I desire you to speak once more to the accused and explain to him in the most forthright terms where his best interest must lie. I shall therefore adjourn this court until to-morrow.'

Welter looked up at the clock and tried to remember the times of the next two trains.

★ ★ ★ ★

The court resumed sitting at 10.30 in the morning. The jury were back in their seats. The judge questioned Welter. 'Have you anything to tell me?'

'I regret not, my lord.'

'Very well.' The judge spoke to the jury.

'The accused has decided to represent himself from now on and to disperse with the services of counsel. In your absence yesterday, I asked the accused to reconsider this decision, deeming it not in his best interests, but he has declined to do so. He has an inalienable right to represent himself here and will therefore do so from now on.'

Julian gave his evidence, as he had given it at the previous trial.

His cross-examination began and after three quarters of an hour Calaghan was questioning him about the empty cartridge case that had been found near the body.

'Do you dispute the fact that the cartridge case was fired from your gun?'

'How can I?'

'Do you dispute the fact that the cartridge case had been fired on the Saturday in question?'

'Once again, how can I?'

'Do you admit to firing your gun on the ride at the spot where this cartridge was found?'

'I do not.'

'How do you explain the fact that the cartridge was found where it was. Unless it came from your gun when you fired at your brother and killed him?'

'I can't explain it. I don't know anything about it. You're only trying me here because I was in trouble before. If I hadn't a previous conviction for manslaughter by shooting...'

'It was clear that this was going to happen,' interrupted the judge. 'Mr Calaghan, have all the necessary inquiries been made?'

'Yes, my lord.'

'With what result?'

'The accused has never before suffered conviction for any crime.'

'Can you call witnesses to that fact?'

'Yes, my lord.'

'Mr Decker,' said the judge, 'full inquiries have been made, making it certain beyond any doubt that you have never suffered conviction for any crime. If you persist in your claim to have suffered such previous conviction, these witnesses will be called to refute your allegation. Do you still wish to maintain that you have been previously convicted of a crime?'

'But I have been.'

'You can do yourself only harm by this. Inevitably, the jury will be led to draw certain conclusions.'

'I'm telling the truth.'

'Mr Calaghan,' said the judge, 'the accused will step down from the witness-box and you will call witnesses as to the facts.'

'I *was* convicted,' shouted Julian. 'In the Congo in nineteen-fifty-seven.'

'The...the Congo?' said the judge.

'I can prove it.'

'How?'

'I have the judgment, signed by the judge.' Julian brought a large brown envelope from his inside pocket.

'Show it to me.'

The usher was instructed to collect the envelope. He carried it across to the clerk of the court who handed it to the Bench. The judge opened the envelope and brought out a single sheet of paper which he unfolded. He read the statement which was in French, typewritten, and on headed paper. He put the paper down and consulted passages in two of his law books. 'Mr Calaghan, under the Act of eighteen-fifty-one, I am obliged to accept this authenticated copy of a judgment since although it bears no seal it specifically states that the court in question has no seal. Further, it purports to be signed by the presiding judge.' It was a forgery, thought the judge, with bitter anger. It was a forgery, but would it be at all easy to prove it so? Surely, most records in the Congo would have been destroyed during that unhappy country's civil wars? If Decker had chosen a date when he could show he was abroad... After all, it was only a suspended sentence which had been imposed on him so that a relatively short absence from England would suffice...

The judge tried to find some way of avoiding what he was obliged to do, but there was no way. He questioned Julian. 'It is my duty to inform you that when an irregularity such as the accidental disclosure of a previous conviction takes place during the trial of an undefended prisoner, that prisoner has the right to apply that the jury be discharged and the trial be started afresh. If you desire to make such application, you must do so forthwith. Do you so desire?'

'I do,' replied Julian.

★ ★ ★ ★

Faced with a prisoner who had, only temporarily it was hoped, discovered a means by which to use the law to frustrate any trial of himself, the authorities took the only possible course open to them. A *nolle prosequi* was entered. Although it was usual to enter such a fiat only where the accused person could not be produced in court to plead owing to physical or mental incapacity, it was held that such an entry could be made to meet the unusual needs in the present instance. The *nolle prosequi* put an end to the proceedings, but did not operate as a bar, a discharge, or an acquittal. Julian would be re-indicted when the law was ready.

CHAPTER 19

Saturday, the 29th of January was a day of contrasts. The sky was cloudless, but the overnight frost had been heavy so that not until late in the morning did the sun melt the white glaze with which everything had been covered. The wind was strong and cold enough to penetrate any amount of clothing and those who were shooting had to choose between being very cold or wearing so many clothes that they could no longer raise their guns easily or swing smoothly.

In the house, Julian and Henry Decker drank coffee very liberally spiced with rum.

'It's going to be hell,' said Julian, 'but the birds will fly really well. Adams says this frost has driven them all into the coverts.'

'Are you having cocks only at most beats?'

'Just a couple, but no more. I did a bit of research and checked the records and to my mind there's no doubt that it doesn't really pay to shoot hens after Christmas. It's only one year in four or five that the wild hens rear decent sized broods and in all the other years the weather kills off the young. I reckon it's much better to shoot the hens right through the season and then put down a few more birds than you would have done. Adams, of course, has accused me of heresy.'

Barbara and Lydia came into the dining-room.

'This house is so cold,' said Lydia. 'I don't think we'll survive. I'm sure it's not healthy to be cold and that's why Eskimos die so young and so easily.'

'They die from T.B and 'flu,' said Julian.

'Nonsense. Germs couldn't possibly live in such cold.'

'Then on your own argument, the cold must be healthy.'

'Julian, you're worse than ever. It doesn't matter what I say, you argue. Your father was quite right when he said you were a born sophist and should have gone into parliament or somewhere equally disreputable. Henry, persuade him to stop arguing.'

Henry Decker laughed. 'I've always been taught that the Deckers are so pig-headed on certain subjects that no one's ever been able to teach them that the alphabet doesn't start at the letter D.'

'That's rather rude, Henry, but not without its merits.'

They heard, distantly, the knocking on the front door.

'That'll be George,' said Julian. 'You know George Younger, don't you, Henry? He's a damn, good shot on his day, although there's never any certainty it's going to be his day. He's coming in in place of...' He stopped suddenly.

The one word 'Fawcett' that had not been spoken reminded them all with a brutal shock that this was not just one more shooting party. Julian was there only because the law had found it could not rectify a fault in its make-up as quickly as it wanted to. Soon, the law would be back for him. In the meantime, it was watching him. Doherty had been along the previous day to check if there was going to be a shoot and had then asked that one of his men be allowed to be around 'just to keep an eye on things.' Angrily, Julian had demanded whether Doherty expected him to shoot someone else? Doherty had just shaken his head.

Barbara stepped close to Julian and took hold of his hand in hers, in a gesture that at the same time was comforting him and appealing to him to comfort her.

George Younger, a tall, thin, spruce man who exactly looked the retired army officer he was, entered the dining-room. He greeted them and gratefully accepted a coffee and rum. 'By God, that wind's got knives in it!' He drank. 'Are there many birds left, Julian?'

'Adams says there are quite a few. That probably means there are a hell of a lot.'

'This wind will lift them up.'

'They'll look like starlings at King's Beat.'

Everyone did his or her best to forget why Julian was there and Fawcett was not.

★ ★ ★ ★

Adams cursed the beaters for a lot of fiddling pikies. 'Beat them brambles out,' he shouted. 'You won't get no birds moving by bashing air.'

'Shall we put salt on their tails?' asked someone.

'You'll do some bloody work or get back home.'

Adams moved forward once more and the line moved with him. He saw a hen pheasant get up seventy yards farther on and fly forward. After a while, he heard the sound of a shot. He cursed Mr Julian's stupid idea of shooting hens at the end of the season. Since time immemorial, no one had shot hens so late because that killed off next season's crop of birds. But Mr Julian had had his brains twisted by someone, had had a look at the records of the estate and added up the wrong figures, and had come to the wrong conclusions. All he, Adams, could do was to try to drive the hens out sideways so that they never went near the guns, but hens were stupid and seemed to want to go forward in direct contrast to the wily old cocks who were forever trying to break sideways.

His dog put up a rabbit that was suffering from the first stages of myxomatosis. It moved away, but directly towards a beater who killed it to put it out of its misery. Some townspeople claimed shooting was cruel, thought Adams, but had they any idea what was inflicted on rabbits in the name of better farming so as to feed them with cheap food?

'Straighten the line,' he called out. Soon, they would be up to the rhododendron bushes and the main flushes. Secretly, he expected a really good drive here.

★ ★ ★ ★

Julian watched a cock pheasant fly out of the woods, gain height with beating wings and then plane. The wind drifted it sharply across to the left of him. It was a testing shot. He automatically slipped the safety catch forward, raised the gun to his shoulder, gauged the curving flight, began the swing behind and inside the curve, swung forward and fired. As the gun recoiled, he saw the pheasant's neck jerk back and both legs drop. The bird arced down to the ground, landing far back in the Larch Plantation. It had been a first-class shot by anyone's standards. He broke the gun and the empty cartridge in the left-handed barrel—he'd used choke—was ejected several feet away. He pulled a fresh cartridge out of the waist belt and inserted it, closed the gun and, as no other bird was coming over, put his hand in his pocket and depressed the plunger of the counter once.

He held the gun at the ready since the big flushes would begin at any moment. A woodcock suddenly and silently appeared, twisting round the branches of a willow with a brilliant display of aerial gymnastics. He fired the right barrel and the left and the woodcock went on its twisting way, unscathed. As he reloaded, two hen pheasants came straight over him. By the time he had closed the gun and turned they were out of range.

He heard the distant sound of beating wings that signified a big flush and a second later the faintly audible order for the beaters to hold. The birds came in sight, rising very steeply with the wind. They approached at various angles and heights, all going like hell riding an express train. He shot one and missed one, broke the gun, and both empty cartridges were ejected. As he pulled two cartridges out of his belt, Henry Decker stepped round a willow tree to come into sight in the small clearing of the stand.

'Run out of cartridges?' asked Julian, as he reloaded. He fired at a cock pheasant and the bird dropped. 'Take some out of the bag. It's just there by the stick.' He broke the gun and the empty cartridge was ejected. As he went to draw a fresh cartridge from his belt, he looked down to see the barrels of Henry Decker's gun pointing at his head. 'Look out...' He stopped, as he realised with a chilling sense of shock that this was no piece of careless gun handling.

Henry Decker slid the safety catch forward with his thumb. As his forefinger curled round the front trigger, there was a loud shout. A man burst through the undergrowth into the clearing.

Henry Decker stood quite motionless.

Julian stared at the twin muzzles of the shotgun and found himself wondering whether the mind had time, before it was blasted out of existence, to record the agonising pain as the column of shot smashed into the flesh.

'Drop that gun,' ordered the man. As Henry Decker hesitated, he threw himself forward.

Henry Decker pulled the trigger. There was no shattering explosion, no cone of shot tearing into Julian's head, only the sharp click of the striker-pin as it hit the cap of the cartridge.

The man crashed into Henry Decker, who was thrown to the ground. Henry Decker struggled to bring the gun round and received two blows in his stomach which left him doubled up in agony.

Julian stared at the man as he came to his feet. 'God! if that cartridge hadn't misfired by some miracle...' he muttered.

The other picked up the gun, broke it, and extracted the right-hand cartridge. 'Luckily, sir, we doctored this one. What worried me was that we hadn't doctored the other.'

★ ★ ★ ★

In Hurstley Place, Doherty sat in the arm-chair to the right of the fireplace in the red withdrawing-room. The blazing fire, made up of two thick sections of tree trunk and any number of smaller ones, threw out just enough heat that reached him to persuade him that he was not too cold. He drank some whisky. On his right, past generations of the Deckers looked down at him from their framed portraits. By the side of the fireplace hung a flintlock pistol: had that one ever faced a horde of starving Irish peasants?

'How in the hell were you able to doctor that one cartridge?' asked Julian. 'You weren't to know which one he'd use.'

'The detective constable made himself useful at the first beat, sir. He got his hand on Henry Decker's cartridge bag and passed it back to me and I changed all the cartridges. Then I weighed the ones from the bag.'

'Weighed them?'

'Yes, sir. I expected to find one slightly lighter than the others and after a while I did. This cartridge had a distinguishing mark on the cap, which was good confirmation.'

'I'm sorry, but I don't see the significance.'

'Well, sir, you'll remember Mr Williams, the gun expert, and the pathologist between them proved that in two cases the murdered man had been shot by the standard load of a number five shot sixteen bore cartridge—which is about two hundred and six pellets. Had the load come from a standard twelve bore cartridge, that number would have been two hundred and thirty-four pellets. You'll know better than me that it's the number of pellets which is important, not the pellets themselves as a number five pellet can come from any bore gun.

'Mr Williams was of the very definite opinion the murderer wouldn't know that the size of cartridge used could be determined by the weight and number of shot, but experts who believe themselves infallible aren't always so very clear when they move from facts to theories. Anyway, according to Williams the murderer used a sixteen bore cartridge and this had obviously either to be fired from a sixteen bore gun—which only you and your brother used—or a twelve bore in which was an adaptor. Not only would this adaptor have been a most unusual one—adaptors normally scale down to a four ten—but it would have been a clumsy method as the murderer would have to carry the adaptor round with him plus a sixteen bore cartridge which, when found, would bear the unique and identifying marks of his own gun. The truth was that the murderer was fully aware of the relevance of the weight and number of pellets in the charge and he hit on the idea of taking a twelve bore cartridge and reducing the number of pellets in it to a sixteen bore load. He could thus safely use his own twelve bore gun to commit the murder and yet make it appear the murder weapon was a sixteen bore.

'When he shot your brother, Henry Decker carried the deception one stage further than he had before. At the first beat he'd pick up from your stand one of the used sixteen bore cartridges which, of course, bore all the identifying marks of your gun on it and after he'd shot your brother with a lightened twelve bore cartridge in his gun, he dropped this sixteen bore case on the ride. That meant there was a cartridge case at the murder spot which could be proved absolutely to have been fired from your gun.

'That all leads up to why I searched for the lightened cartridge this morning. When I found it, I gave the detective constable, a similar cartridge of the correct weight and with the identifying mark. He introduced it into Henry Decker's cartridge bag.'

Julian finished his drink. 'Another?'

'I'm always ready for a drop more whisky, sir, even when it's Scotch and not Irish.'

Julian poured out the drinks. 'Why? Why did he kill?' He returned to his chair after handing the other a glass and sat down.

'This case, sir, has been cursed from the beginning by the wrong conclusions being drawn from the right facts. And it's no consolation at all to know that we were meant to draw those wrong conclusions.

'This estate is worth at least half a million pounds and a lot of men will do anything to get a fortune like that. Henry Decker was a Decker and yet he wasn't. Since your mutual grandfather married twice and had a son by each marriage, you and your brother were the direct descendents of the elder son and in line to inherit the estate, Henry Decker was the son of the younger son and not in line, although the eldest of the three of you. He would never come into the estate worth half a million pounds. He always saw it as a sum of money, not as you and your brother saw it, the permanent inheritance of the family and not belonging to any single member of that family.

'Greed and envy twisted his mind and every time he came here and smilingly thanked you for whatever hospitality you'd just given him, that envy dug deeper and hurt more. You two had inherited everything, he had inherited nothing but a nagging, bad tempered wife. He was a Decker, yet the name meant nothing. He was the oldest of the generation, yet the half million pound estate would never come to him.

'Your father set up the trust fund and this became effective so that the estate was saved from death duties and was due to vest in your brother or yourself, depending on your brother's decision when he reached thirty-five. One day, Henry Decker suddenly realised a truth that until then had escaped him: there were only two lives between him and the half million, since your mother had signed away any and all of her rights when the trust was formed. Of those two lives, your brother was living on borrowed time and would almost certainly elect against accepting the estate. That reduced the number to one—you.

'He's admitted that he day-dreamed how to kill you if and when your brother died. Then, out of the blue, he learned that Rafferty was blackmailing you because your father had, in fact, died before the five years was up. This meant that if ever the truth came out, death duties would be levied on the estate and crush it out of existence.

'Rafferty blackmailed you for two reasons. He hated you for what he took to be your snobbish superiority, and he was determined to force you to socially receive him and his wife. By blackmailing you he could hurt you and there's nothing more satisfying than hurting someone one envies. When it came to this blackmail, Henry Decker was more of a realist than ever anyone in your family was. You were prepared to pay the asking price for Rafferty's silence: that was, the money he'd take because it was proof he was hurting you, and the invitation to the house. But Henry Decker knew that there's never any end to blackmail. Rafferty would have gone on blackmailing you and quite soon he would have realised how much more he could squeeze out of you than he was: although, unusually, the money didn't initially interest him as money, he would very soon have understood that he had gained access to half a million pounds. Henry Decker knew that if the estate was to be saved, Rafferty—and Abbotts his gross shadow—had to be dealt with. But why should he worry about saving the estate when he could have no interest in its salvation?

'It was at this point that he realised he would gain an interest.

'He would murder Rafferty and Abbotts and make their deaths appear to be accidents. He'd take every possible precaution, but obviously something could always go wrong. Therefore, he'd shoot them with cartridges whose load had been reduced to sixteen bore loads since only you and your brother used sixteen bores.

'When he killed your brother, he made certain it was obviously murder. He shot him from a distance. He dropped the game counter in a turn-up and an empty cartridge case down on the ride. The motive for this murder was going to be obvious—in just one month your brother was going to make the election which could disinherit you completely. It was Henry Decker's luck that you happened to be on the ride at the right time for his plan, but his plan would have worked just as well had you not been there, looking for a dead fox.'

Julian drained his glass. 'How the hell did all this get him any nearer the estate? I was still very much alive.'

'You were, and with your brother dead the estate would automatically come to you. But there's a law, quoted at your trial, which says that no man may benefit from his crime. If you were found guilty of shooting your brother, you could not inherit the estate: the law would deny you the fruits of your murder. In that case, since the trust had become intestate, as it were, the estate would pass to the nearest relative. Although only a cousin of the half blood, Henry Decker would take under the share that would have gone to his father, had his father still been alive—which meant the whole thing.

'Boiled down, it meant he'd found a way to deprive you of your inheritance by making the law work for him.'

Julian stood up. 'I'm still thirsty. Are you?'

'I probably shouldn't be, sir, but I am.'

Julian poured out fresh drinks. 'What about the counter?'

'He'd pinched that out of the gun-room when he first arrived at the house. After each beat, he must casually have asked you how many birds you'd shot, then clicked up the number. At King's Beat he couldn't see you, but he could see the birds in the air and note how many dropped over your stand and that's how he got the right figure on the counter when he dropped it into the turn-up of your brother's trousers.

'When we investigated Raffery's death we thought it probably wasn't an accident: when we investigated Abbott's death we were certain that that couldn't be an accident. What's more, the killings had to be connected. After a bit, we found what obviously was the connection. Your father had died within the five year period, Rafferty had found this out and had been blackmailing you. He and Abbotts were murdered to save the estate from having to pay the death duties it would have to pay if the true date of your father's death became known. It seemed the murderer had to be you or your brother. Then your brother was killed within a month of his thirty-fifth birthday, when he'd have to make his election. That month was obviously of the greatest importance and we thought it could only be of importance to you. But it was also of supreme importance to Henry Decker because if your brother once elected not to take the estate and you inherited it, you could no longer be deprived of it by the rule against benefiting from your crime.'

Julian lit a cigarette. He was silent for a while, then asked: 'What happens to me?'

'I'm not quite certain how they'll go about your trial now, sir. Maybe after one of those things called a *nolle prosequi* they can just declare you completely innocent.'

'Will they go for Miss Harmsworth over that judgment I claimed came from the Congo?'

'My guess is they'll be happy to forget everything. After all, there are a few red faces around, including mine! We don't want to make them any redder.' He smiled, finished his drink, and stood up. 'I really must be moving, sir.'

They walked from the red withdrawing-room through to the hall. Doherty looked round at all the heraldic shields. 'D'you know something, sir, I reckon that what all this represents is one of the precious things this country has to offer. I suppose that makes me a hopeless square.'

'If so, we're both equally hopeless.'

Doherty went to the front door and opened it. 'Thanks again,' Julian said.

'Good-bye, sir. Oh, by the way, this fell out of Mr Henry Decker's pocket. I think you would probably like to have it.' Doherty handed Julian an envelope. Doherty smiled and then went across the porch to his car.

Julian closed the door, turned, and looked at the hall. Around the walls was much of the history of the Deckers, a history that must now partially end. Henry Decker had failed to get the estate for himself, but in failing he had made certain it did not remain with the Deckers. The police knew the true date of the elder Fawcett's death and already they probably had proof of that date. The state would demand its death duties: the age of unequal equality would have won one more Pyrrhic victory.

He looked down at the envelope Doherty had given him and opened it. Inside was some sort of document, in French, which was both signed and witnessed. He read it. Doctor Roget admitted the deception that had been practised in respect of the death of the Englishman, Monsieur Fawcett Decker. The actual date of death was the 10th of June.

Julian stared at the statement, afraid to believe that he really held it in his hands. Henry Decker had taken it from Rafferty after the first murder and Doherty had somehow, unseen, taken it from Henry Decker after the arrest. Doherty believed in history and so had given it to Julian, not the State.

He went over to the fire, threw the paper on to it, and watched it burn. When there was only a blackened, curling mass left he smashed that into minute fragments with a long handled poker.

Barbara walked into the hall. 'Has he gone?'

'Yes.' He watched one of the fragments as it was wafted up the enormous open chimney by the rising hot air.

'Julian, I don't know whether I'm going to laugh or cry, or what.' She came up and took hold of him, seeking the comfort and reassurance of physical contact. She stared at the fire. 'What were you burning when I came in?'

'Doctor Roget's sworn statement about the date of father's death.'

'But...but how?'

'The detective inspector gave it to me just before he left.'

She began to cry. 'I'm being very feminine,' she murmured after a short while. 'I'm crying because I'm so happy I don't know what else to do. Julian—is Hurstley safe?'

'They'll never be able to prove the real date of father's death now.'

'Why did the detective do it? Why didn't he hand it in?'

'He's a traditionalist. I think he wanted our son's shield to join the rest.'

'Then hadn't we better hurry up and get married, Julian, or there'll be one of those terrible things on it called a bar sinister?'

The publishers hope that this book has given you enjoyable reading. Large Print Books are especially designed to be as easy to see and hold as possible. If you wish a complete list of our books, please ask at your local library or write directly to: Dales Large Print, Long Preston, North Yorkshire, BD23 4ND, England.

Other DALES Mystery Titles In Large Print

PETER CHAMBERS
Somebody Has To Lose

PETER ALDING
A Man Condemned

ALAN SEWART
Plight Of The Innocents

RODERIC JEFFRIES
The Benefits Of Death

MARY BRINGLE
Murder Most Gentrified

JAMES HADLEY CHASE
Get A Load Of This

EVELYN HARRIS
Largely Trouble